Bloodstained Mirror

Confessions of a Diamond Smuggler

Paul Nichols Paula Emery

Tony grew up in a quiet, suburban town called Weatherpool. It was nestled in the foothills of a set of inlets and woodlands and was permeated with lush greenery and rivers that meandered through the wooden conclaves into boggy swamps and deep ponds. The town was split down the middle by the River Weather, which came deep from inland and flowed out to meet the jagged cliffs and into the salty deep blue waters that bathed the feathery white, sandy beaches.

The houses were a prominent feature of Weatherpool. Visitors to the town would see that each one was grander than the one they'd seen before, until they reached those further up into town, ostentatious and huge, with a view to die for.

Each house was a statement about its dwellers. Driveways expressed their flamboyancy with luxurious Lamborghinis and priceless vintage cars and the gardens were preened and groomed as if they were being entered into a flower competition. There was no shame in the fact that one of those houses was Tony's family home.

The rear gardens of most of the homes backed onto a waterway. Those that didn't have access could reach the rivers by using private footpaths or makeshift roads, which had become a main route for trespassers over time. Most families were linked to fisheries in one way or another; some caught fish and some came for the mysterious angel dust in the salty waters. Although everyone was aware of the fact that substances were trafficked on those waterways, no one dared speak about it. Most knew why people here were so wealthy. Speedboats were moored at the end of gardens and, although they were mostly brand new, strangely, they would undergo major internal and external refurbishment after returning from 10-day trips. Sadly, Tony's family weren't interested in fishing or boats.

Most of these gardens had a shallow cave, a man-made borehole, or a shaft that was used to store equipment for their boats. Why not just use a normal shed to store such things, you might ask?

The truth is, there were much more malevolent reasons for having such caves and boreholes.

Approximately 40,000 people lived in Weatherpool and the nearby city of Portland, which is the kind of number you'd expect at a concert or football match. In some way or other, most people knew someone from all the different families that lived there, even if they didn't know every individual. Most Portland and Weatherpool visitors would describe the town as a tourists' paradise; however, to the locals, the place had a very different feel. People who lived there were bored by the fake serenity and took little notice of the vague beauty; their lives were punctuated by multiple murders and the mysterious missing members of families.

There were two distinct groups in the relatively opulent community: the 'haves' (the wealthy) and the 'have-nots' (the deprived). The 'haves' were related to the mafia, demented drug entrepreneurs, and reformed ex-convicts. The 'have-nots' were career-driven brainiacs who had spent years in various colleges and universities, striving to find the next invention or attempting to become 'professional'. The former group were very much talked about. The latter were of no interest to the local gossipers.

Tony is a professional but isn't afraid to push the boundaries of danger and takes unimaginable risks; for this reason, his family are borderline 'haves'.

Nicky and Tony first met when they were nine years old and still in primary school and their ideas chimed perfectly from the start of their friendship. Nicky lived in an area nicknamed 'Free Port'. Ironically, nothing about it was free. It was approximately five kilometres west of Weatherpool, roughly a 20-minute drive; it was also near the town centre of Portland. Free Port was renowned for gun-hiring opportunities and, for the right price, someone would think nothing of ridding you of your foes. That 'someone' would not necessarily be an adult. Recently, Free Port visitors had reported seeing youths as young as eleven casually walking around with a pistol poking out from their waistbands. Nicky's grandmother, now deceased, often spoke of the days that she, too, strapped a gun to her upper thigh under her school dress. She did this for her brothers when they passed police checkpoints. She said, 'Who would search a nine-year-old girl in school uniform'?

Free Port was like a ghost town. If you didn't already live there, you probably wouldn't want to venture in. In fact, visitors weren't really welcomed at all. However, because of their families' status in Free Port, and because Nicky and Tony were friends, Tony was able to come and go as he pleased, although he was often expected to pay the bar tabs for well-known gangs. Tony was known as 'Teach' by the locals and it was sometimes difficult for him to actually get to Nicky's house because he'd be intercepted *en route*. Nicky's home was a two-bedroom detached house, left to him by his late father. On the same compound, two other houses stood, now occupied by his mother and younger siblings. His grandmother lived in another house on the opposite side of the yard. Nicky's house was cosy, with an open-plan diner and kitchen on the ground floor, along with a small guest bedroom. Upstairs was a master bedroom, bathroom, and patio, which was originally planned for an extension for a third bedroom. This idea was abandoned when Nicky's dad fell ill. On the substantial yard out front were parked Nicky's blue, white and red Honda CBR 600 and his Ford F-150 pickup. Other vehicles were littered across the yard too. They were stored there until they could be sold on at the garage owned by Nicky's uncle and his brother in Free Port.

Behind the landscape was a malodorous mix of something musty – perhaps urine and decay. The source of the stench was a swamp 500 metres from Nicky's house, the direction of which was clear from the frequently, but secretly, trodden footpaths. The yard's wide range of vehicles, most of which were reconditioned or crash repairs, offered opportunities for test drives. They were all of a very high standard and were usually sold on really quickly. Often, the vehicles were customised with hidden compartments under the seats or in the engine. Due to this reconditioning service, Nicky's uncle and his brother were infamous in certain quarters.

You might wonder why someone like Tony, a teacher from a reasonable affluent background, would be associated with such people in Free Port. As a child, his mentors were not so academically inclined. He grew up with respect for the sophisticated criminal gangs in his neighbourhood. While studying for his BA honours degree he had concurrently studied the 'art of criminality' at a more 'local level'. He observed famous gangs, secretly waiting to take over Nicky's patch. Tony had always attracted a certain type of associate: those with wealth and a colourful and non-legitimate lifestyle. When he had not long turned nineteen, Tony met a female politician who was heavily connected with credit card fraud. She was raking in millions of dollars through card cloning. Ironically, she was married to a senior police officer who provided mules to carry out the transactions, but that's a different story.

Tony's day often starts with a six kilometre run around a carefully mapped circuit of Weatherpool. He follows that with six repetitions of fifty push-ups and two hundred abdominal crunches, an oatmeal breakfast with egg or avocado, jalapeños, and sun dried tomatoes on toast. This is before he starts his working day, during which he teaches five classes of twenty-two children, whose education is entrusted to him. He does enjoy imparting knowledge upon these impressionable young people; however, teaching is just not rewarding enough. He is very aware that he can make millions of dollars if the right people decide they want to use his intellect to formulate a 'not-so-educational' plan.

After class on one particular day, Tony

planned to meet with his trusted buddy, Nicky Vernon. Nicky was like a brother to him and was a musician and poet. They knew each other so well that, sometimes, they finished each other's sentences. Often, just by looking at each other, they, scarily, knew what the other was thinking. They were as deeply in tune as brothers could be. Nicky also had a daily exercise routine, but his was harder, longer, and more intense. Nicky was stronger, more agile, and more robust than his friend. He looked like a cage fighter (minus the tattoos) with his long black curly hair, which he always wore in a ponytail.

It was a sunny Tuesday afternoon. The two men had arranged to meet at their favourite Chinese restaurant for a late lunch. They wanted to update each other on their plans and set the major task, which they had been training for over the last month, into motion. Tony often seemed to meet unscrupulous people and today was no different. Standing in the middle of the footpath, which led from the school grounds to the area where the restaurant was located, stood a man. He was averagely built and dressed in a scruffy grey and blue shirt, too big and hanging loosely as if he was a rag doll that a child had dressed in their own clothing. As Tony got closer, he noticed the man was agitated. He was poking about in his wallet as though he'd lost its contents. He looked up, and with a frown he watched Tony approaching. He seemed to jump into action as if he'd been prodded and spoke with a croaky voice.

'Hi, Teach'. He covered his mouth with the back of his hand. He repeated, 'Teach?'

'Hey,' said Tony, hesitantly.

'Teach!' he said louder, as he realised that Tony was going to walk past. 'You wouldn't happen to have a twenty or so spare that I could borrow?'

Tony had no idea who this man was but he obviously knew him. He stopped walking and turned to the man. He was just going to answer his question, but the man interrupted …

'You might not remember me – I'm Dwayne Martin's dad. I used to work at Brinks security. I came to parents evening in my uniform. Remember?'

'Oh yes,' said Tony. 'I remember Dwayne.' He

paused, then said, 'I don't remember seeing him in school for a very long time.'

The man looked at his feet, and mumbled quietly, 'Dwayne has leukaemia. He's very ill. He's just come out of hospital after treatment.'

Tony felt like he'd been slapped across the face. 'Oh my God, I'm so sorry to hear that!'

The man continued to tell Tony that Dwayne had limited time left. He explained that he'd lost his job at Brinks and was struggling to pay his bills. He didn't mentioned Dwayne's mother in all of this, using 'I' not 'we'. Tony wondered whether she had left when she was most needed.

'I'm truly sorry to hear about Dwayne,' said Tony. He looked through his own Montblanc wallet, but realised he had no cash.

Tony looked at the man apologetically. 'I'm on my way to a restaurant to meet a friend. There's an ATM nearby. Walk with me and I'll get some cash out for you.'

The man's eyes lit up and his face beamed. 'Thanks Teach. Dwayne always spoke highly of you!' With that, he coughed, covering his mouth with his hand, which was now splattered with phlegm. He tried to speak, but could only manage, 'I re-ally … cough … prec … iate … cough, cough … your kind … cough … ness.' He reached out with his splattered hand to show his appreciation with a handshake. Tony instinctively shoved his hands into his own pockets, pretending to look for cash that he knew wasn't there.

The two men walked together along the footpath. As they walked, they continued their conversation about Dwayne and how he, Daniel, and the rest of the family, were coping. Lack of money obviously amplified their problems. It was clear to Tony that Daniel looked after his son the best he could but that meant being at home most of the time. Daniel showed his frustration and annoyance about his work dismissal.

'If I had my way, I would rob one of the Brinks trucks on its cash collection rounds.'

Tony told Daniel that it would probably not be the best plan he'd ever had. 'That would lead to a lot of bloodshed,' warned Tony. 'The trucks are heavily guarded.'

They exited the footpath onto Dorchester Road. Tony saw Nicky waiting at the entrance to the restaurant a few metres away. Tony shouted to him to get his attention, then he and Daniel weaved their way across the road through the slow-moving traffic.

Nicky looked quizzically at Tony as if to say, 'Who the hell is this guy?'

'Hi bro! This is Daniel,' shouted Tony. Seeing the frown on Nicky's face, Tony said, 'I will explain in a minute,' then walked off to the ATM, leaving the two men standing together awkwardly.

Tony hastily withdrew a paltry sum of twenty dollars out of the cash machine and dashed back over to Daniel, who took the money with a beaming smile of gratitude. He thanked Tony, bowed his head, and rushed desperately away to buy necessities from the local supermarket.

Nicky and Tony walked into the restaurant, where they were greeted amicably by familiar staff and guided to their favourite table at the back of the huge room. They ordered their favourites – seaweed, frog's legs in black bean sauce, and special fried rice. They quenched their thirst with beer from

Shanghai while they waited on their food; Tony took the opportunity to explain the situation with Daniel. He told him about Dwayne and the family's financial situation; he also mentioned what Daniel had said about robbing the Brinks security truck. Tony sniggered about this, but Nicky's face turned deadly serious at the thought.

'Tony ...' he said, lowering his tone. 'We might be onto something here. We should explore this. A while back, I met a Brinks security truck driver. According to him, every Friday, the Brinks trucks transferred between thirteen and twenty three million dollars from the Central Bank to a cargo plane at the main airport.' He went on to explain that the money was taken by air to be deposited in a special vault.

The conversation continued throughout the evening. They chewed over a plan to convince Daniel to work with them on what they expected to be a bullet-proof project.

Tony pointed out, 'Daniel is desperate for money, so if our plan is watertight, I'm sure he'll go along with it ...' However, before he could go any further, Nicky interrupted, 'I will talk to Uncle

Darren. He knows a lot of people who will get this to work. We will have to be clinical about it. No room for error in surgery!' he joked.

A job like this would entail printing counterfeit bank notes, stacking and binding them, then placing them into special sealed polyethylene bags so they could be swapped out by the Brinks team on the way to the airport. The only money boarding that cargo plane would be counterfeit.

It sounded easy on paper, but it wouldn't be. It was a crazy plan with little substance and not much chance of materialising, but it was the kind of plan that the two friends thrived upon. They craved challenges and, for Tony, teaching a bunch of kids at the local high school was not cutting it. Neither was Nicky's literary and music work giving him the stimulation or satisfaction that his mental capacity required.

'Ok ... let's sleep on this,' said Tony, smiling.

'Agreed,' Nicky replied, excitedly.

Changing the subject, Nicky exclaimed, 'Hey, Teach. Guess who I saw earlier today!?'

'Umm ... you'll have to give me a clue,' replied

Tony. 'I'm sure you've seen many people.'

'Ok, well here's a clue ... she's a blast from our past.'

'Now you've got me thinking ...' mused Tony. 'Go on, tell me ...'

Nicky laughed. 'Grace!!'

The two men both laughed. 'Grace?? Wow!' spluttered Tony.

Grace was definitely a blast for their very distant past. She was one of Tony's and Nicky's first loves at primary school. They were nine years old when Grace was introduced to their class. Her beautiful brown hair and hazy green eyes took the boys' breath away. Even if they were sick with flu, most of the boys in the class still wanted to go to school, just to see Grace.

The ironic thing is that Grace was hardly ever at school. She was absent much of the time and quite clueless when she attended. They often called her the 'pretty dunce'. Regardless of her academic deficiencies, Nicky and Tony spent a lot of time with her. Even at age nine the two boys took turns 'courting' her. They would role play mums and dads in the high fern bushes at the edge of the school's playing field. Grace was the queen and the boys took turns being her charming king.

Nicky and Tony eventually decided that Grace was not for them. On many occasions she seemed to want extraordinary attention. Very often, she told them to kiss her directly on her lips. The boys knew they weren't even allowed to watch kissing scenes in movies, so they were confused as to why they should be kissing a girl in the fern bushes at school.

As time went on, Grace got bored of Nicky and Tony 'playing around' and she moved onto the older boys. She had got fed up with the smell of fern and chasing butterflies and, she knew the older boys would know what came after kissing. Before they left primary school, Grace's mother committed suicide and she left the school. It was later rumoured that her stepdad abused her mother and sexually molested Grace. Sadly, that explains her actions, the basis of which were out of her control and completely unimaginable. She is now a mother herself, in a complex relationship and with a misguided personality.

Nicky's encounter with Grace brought back

memories of the friends' troubled experiences and their many challenging situations, all of which had made their friendship unbreakable. The men continued dining and talking about other their other, future exploits. The main reason for their meeting today was to put the finishing touches to a plan to steal eight kilograms of uncut cocaine from the Saunders' garden well. The Saunders were one of the main, and most dangerous, drug entrepreneur families in Weatherpool, so they needed to decide on the safest way to go about it. Over time, Nicky and Tony had become quite industrious and resourceful when gathering detailed information about the inner workings of different households in their neighbourhoods. To this end, they had intimate encounters with many of the women in the towns and in several neighbouring towns and cities. They weren't particular with whom they were intimate. The women could be aged nineteen or ninety. It didn't matter, it just had to be done.

Their plan to confiscate Mr Saunders' hidden stash of cocaine was at an advanced stage. Tony had surreptitiously gathered information about the contents of the Saunders' garden well and property two weeks earlier, during pillow talk with Mr Saunders' sister-in-law, Eszter Skai. This was not to be taken lightly. She was hard work to talk to and was repugnant, fat, and didn't like to shower or shave. However, again, it had to be done.

They'd prepared everything they needed to complete the mission the day before. The Saunders' house was only a few minutes' walk from Tony's house. Therefore, not only was this task high stake, personal, and local, it was also incredibly stupid. After their meal, the friends took a taxi to Tony's house in Weatherpool, making sure that the driver took them up to the side of the house, so they could enter via the back door. They waited until nightfall before venturing out through that same door into Tony's back garden then through a small opening into a wooded area that carried on to the waterway. They both wore forest-green skin-tight diving suits with extra padding on the forearms, complemented by two camouflage backpacks and thick green rubber gloves.

In their shoulder bags were four makeshift hilts, made from six-inch corrugated steel and sharpened, complete with rubber handles; two whole chickens, chopped into bloody bitesize chunks; two four kilogram packs of ammonium nitrate fertiliser in refuse bags; and a fifteen centimetre garden spade, wire, a lock cutter, and two two-way radios with earpieces.

The Saunders' plush eight-bedroom house, kitted out with a Jacuzzi, greenhouse, and swimming pool was very inviting. The garden propagated the riverbank, like most of the houses in the town. At the end of the swimming pool, stood an outdoor bar and kitchenette, with a storeroom affixed. The Well was contiguous with the back of the shed and approximately two and half metres of the shed roof was hanging over it. There were two contorted ropes dangling from the ceiling of the overhanging roof, probably left there after a lynching. For additional security, two imperilling black Rottweilers were anchored on either side of the garden well, seemingly to dissuade any would-be burglars. The two beastly looking Rottweilers were fed daily on a diet of undercooked meat, to ensure that the taste of blood-drenched flesh didn't become extraneous to them.

Nicky and Tony had to stake out the

Saunders' for just under two hours, watching the house from the greenery that overlooked their garden. This was the area of woodland that Tony had looked out at many times through his female consort's bedroom window. Nicky and Tony held two positions, like well-trained assassins. While Tony lay low watching the house from the fern bushes, Nicky stayed under the covering of a tree, two hundred meters further back, keeping an eye on his conspirator who was in the sentry position. They waited until nightfall when all of the household had left to go on a night out, just as Eszter had said.

Through his earpiece, Tony heard Nicky's voice. 'It's time, let's go ...'

Under darkness, they made their way towards the chain-linked fence crowned and plaited with barbed wire. They had to be quick, careful, and absolutely silent. Tony remained motionless as he waited for Nicky to arrive at his position, three metres away from the fence, which ran parallel to the swimming pool.

They moved stealthily towards the fence. It was no surprise that the dogs started to growl. Nicky and Tony looked at each other and Nicky whispered, 'Have they smelt the blood-drenched chicken ... or us ... or both?'

They grinned at each other and then turned to focus on the next stage of their mission. Nicky began cutting through the wire fence. It took him less than thirty seconds to cut through one metre, enough for the teacher to push his head and shoulders through the gap.

'Go on Teach! I've got this ... you first and then do the same for me,' Nicky whispered. He used his gloved left hand to pull away the fence to create a gap wide enough for Tony's upper torso to slide through. Tony held onto the opposite edge of the wire fence and pulled himself forward. The barbed wire scraped against his right hip as he dragged himself through to the other side. Brushing off the stinging pain, Tony returned the favour. Nicky got through faster than Tony and was standing next to him in no time. They carefully dragged their backpacks through the gap then hurried quietly towards the back of the shed.

Nicky whispered again ... 'Are you taking out

the dog on the right or the one on the left?'

'The one on the right is mine!' muttered Tony. It was natural that Tony should gravitate to the right as he was right handed and much stronger on that side, which would give him an advantage. Nicky was left-handed, so taking the animal on the left suited him.

They were now at the back of the shed and could see one of the muscular Rottweilers barking furiously. Tony reached into his backpack and grabbed the parcel of raw chicken and tossed it towards the animal. Like a circus-trained beast, the huge canine jumped and caught the meat in its enormous jaws. The other beast tried to rush over, but its chain yanked it back to its anchored position. Tony looked around, but couldn't see where Nicky had moved to. 'Where are you, mate?' Nicky replied, 'I'm here ... I can see you.'

Tony slid his backpack to the ground and peered through the darkness towards the corner of the shed, where he could just make out Nicky's shadowy crouching figure. From his side of the well, Tony could hear the dogs crunching through the raw chicken bones. Before they were finished, the two men simultaneously tossed two more portions of chicken towards them, reached into the rucksack for a blade and strode quickly and silently towards them. The dogs, distracted by the meat, were approached from behind. They snarled with each gluttonous bite they took using their immense jaws.

Their movements and timing had to be precise and synchronised. There couldn't be any hesitation. Tony launched himself into a frenzied attack on the dog. Blood oozed from the Rottweiler's ribcage as the corrugated steel penetrated its firm muscular body. It snarled and yelped as it resisted Tony's grip and turned, frantically biting into his rubber jumpsuit. He felt its teeth piercing his skin. His next gouges had to be decisive and final. Holding the raging animal's leg with his left hand, his blade penetrated its neck and then its throat, with several aggressive slashes. The beast's growls silenced, its resistance lessened, and it slumped to the ground. As Tony lay next to the dead animal, he heard his dad's voice and, once again, he became that five-year-old boy struggling with life and death, thinking back to the light in the ceiling reminiscent of the reflection of the bloodstained mirror.

'Teach ...', said a ringing voice in Tony's earpiece. 'Let's get this thing done.'

Tony looked up and could see that Nicky was already standing at the entrance to the well with the lock cutter. He vaulted into an upright position, looking around slightly dazed; he could see a bulging bin bag tied up in the area where the other animal was anchored. Its collar was still attached to the lead, but the dog was not. 'Hey, you extinguished yours quickly!' Tony panted, as he reflected on the length of time he must have spent struggling to slaughter the beast. Nicky must have been much more efficient in his execution.

The snapping of the padlock on the well's door prompted Tony into action. As he grabbed and removed the bin bag from his backpack, his emotions swung back to excitement. Bagging up the dead dog was like loading a bale of hay into a sack; it took a lot of effort. Turning around to move the deadweight out of view, Tony saw the that light from the well was shining like a torch onto the overhanging roof.

The pit was obviously more sophisticated than they had imagined. Maybe it was called a well because it was underground, but, in reality, it was more like a covert house, the length of which ran the full distance of the shed. Its walls and floor were covered with varnished pinewood, decorated with fishing tackle, and there was a stairwell leading underground. This is where they hoped to extricate eight kilograms of angel dust.

'Come on, Teach!' called out Nicky's insistent voice. 'You're in first!'

Tony's heart was pounding as he braced himself and entered the crypt.

'Wow, it's huge! Where do we start?' he exclaimed.

Nicky replied, thoughtfully, 'Something this valuable should be in a safe … or a locked cabinet … so, let's start with anything that's got a lock on it.'

Like prisoners breaking out of their cells, lock after lock snapped. As the padlocks for each cupboard was broken, Tony peered inside. They were starting to wonder whether there was anything to find, when they came across a cash box with two extra locks.

'This is worth looking into,' Nicky said softly.

It required a hammer or crowbar to get it open. Typically, the friends hadn't brought either but there were plenty of tools around them they could improvise with.

Nicky grabbed a hammer and started to smash it against the up-tilted box, knowing that time was against them. It felt like they'd been on this mission for hours, but, in reality, it was only fifteen minutes since they had squeezed through the hole in the fence.

CRASH! Coins and cash fell from the broken tin onto the pinewood floor, which flew open to reveal its treasure of bank notes and a bag of white powder. This was an unexpected surprise; they looked at each other dazed. They had met partial success, but they had to run before the Saunders' arrived home. They would probably check on their guard dogs before retiring to bed. It would be pandemonium when they discovered that their dogs were missing or, worse still, dead.

The two commando-like figures quickly bagged their find and headed back to the stairwell that led from the well up to the back garden, where the two dead animals were awaiting their burial. Their excitement was immeasurable as they looked at each other.

This treasure certainly equated to more than eighty thousand dollars along with the powdery substance that obviously had its own value. All they had to do was get out safely before the Saunders family returned home. If they didn't, they would be killed for sure.

With their rucksacks saddled on their backs, they approached the dead beasts; squatting, and with both hands outstretched, they began to scoop up the animals.

'Fuck!!!' Tony yelled, dropping his hands. 'It's still alive!!'

He felt a huge lump in his throat and started to shake, gasping in disbelief.

'Teach, get a grip!!' said a sobering voice. 'I will take yours … you carry mine. Come on, we don't to be safe.

'Wow!' gasped Tony. 'This looks really good ... have you counted it? How much is it?!'

Nicky reached for his glass and had a sip, before pointing to the chair opposite, gesturing for Tony to sit down.

'It's all been counted and double checked by our banking executive!' he smirked as both men looked towards the kitchen at his girlfriend, Marianna. She was making homemade lasagne. Nicky really had chosen well. Not only was Marianna an Italian beauty, she could also cook *and* she worked in a bank. Tony imagined that if he'd fallen in love, it would be with a woman like Marianna, whose hips and posterior had a status all of their own. The three friends were like family; she would wear whatever she wanted whilst Tony was at the house. Today was no exception; she was dressed in nothing but a small t-shirt and what appeared to be a thong.

'Well according to our banking executive – Miss Italy – we have one hundred and ten thousand, five hundred, and ninety-seven dollars; but there's a question mark on the value of the angel dust.'

Considering their planning and execution, this was the friends' best day in their fifteen-year partnership. They stretched forward with their hands, grasping each other's right thumbs in a congratulatory brotherly handshake. It was Tony's turn to say to thanks to Nicky for supporting him when he needed him the most. It hadn't been easy, and last night's events revealed that his life was still punctuated by underlying issues from his childhood.

Nevertheless, it wasn't a time for Tony to feel sorry for himself. He needed, as did Nicky, to recover without delay. Tony should have been teaching today, but the way he felt, it would be at least a couple of days before he could go back to work. Their biggest concern was the repercussions from the events at the Saunders' property. It was clear that the family would not get the police involved, but someone would have to pay.

'S'cuse me,' Marianna said softly, as she stood over the two men with steaming plates of lasagne. The white sauce was trickling gently down the delicate layers of the stacked pasta, mince, and tell her I cut my arm in an accident on the sport field. I'll just have to keep her busy.' Tony winked at Nicky and Marianna and eased himself gingerly to his feet, loosening up as he walked through their home to their clean laundry pile, where he found some of his clothing. Tony often stayed there so there was always some of his items of clothing mixed in with their laundry; this time it was some shorts and a polo shirt. Bidding them goodbye, he grabbed and put on his trainers, which he'd also left there on a previous visit, and set off, gently at first, but building up speed as his aching body eased into the movement. At a reasonable pace, he would be home within fifty minutes. Tony's family house was nestled along the same riverbank as the Saunders', but nearly three kilometres further upstream, where the water was not deep enough for boats to be moored. There were several coves along the River Weather where, on warm clear days, people would meet up for impromptu shoreline parties.

The riverbanks became narrower and the river was more shallow the further upstream travelled. This meant that, at some points, it was possible to walk close to the bank where the water would only be waist deep.

The deepest part of the river that could be reached from the end of Tony's garden was under two metres deep on a fair day, but when it rained this could reach three metres, which was good for swimming. The waterways teamed with all sorts of wonderful water creatures that could be caught and eaten at barbecues. Very often, people would park their vehicles along the roads that ran parallel to various sections of the river, just to take in the beauty of its nature, or to catch fish.

Tony's house wasn't as aristocratic as the Saunders', or others for that matter, but it boasted seven modestly decorated bedrooms (four en-suite), plus two bedrooms that shared a bathroom and an open-plan, one-bedroom basement apartment. There were also two lounge areas, one of which was used as an entertainment room, whilst the other comprised an adjoining lounge with a Jacuzzi. There was also a grand kitchen and dining hall. The property was split over two and a half floors, the basement being the half. Tony's older brother, Everton, occupied the basement apartment, which was kitted out with a state-of-the-art music system. It was also soundproof with contemporary furnishings. The delicate colour scheme with its white ceiling, brown and green walls, and neutral furniture, had a calming effect, which made you feel like you'd been locked away from the evils of the world.

Everton was hardly ever at home, either because of his girlfriend, April, or because of work. Tony often used his apartment a bit like a brothel. Nicky also brought a 'friend' or two there from time to time. Everton didn't mind, as long as it was kept clean, fresh, and tidy after use.

As he jogged home, it played on Tony's mind that Eszter might be lying to him and that he could be walking into a trap. It was possible that her brother-in-law, Mr Saunders, knew that he and Nicky had broken into their borehole and was using Eszter to get information from Tony to catch him out. 'Well, I'm using Eszter too', Tony murmured to himself, laughing quietly.

There was an eerie silence en route and noticeable posters for information about a missing person. It was an unusual time of day for Tony to be jogging past the Saunders' place to get to his house; on this occasion, he was overwhelmed with fear. He kept a straight head as he ran along the pavement where the Saunders' limestone fence stretched the full length of their dwelling. Six minutes later, he was at home – out of breath – but alive.

Entering the garden through the automatic gate, he made his way to the kitchen and then through the narrow hallway that led to the basement apartment. Tony needed to get ready for Eszter's arrival, physically and mentally. He heard a notification on his phone; she had sent him a text message. It said, 'I will bring a ladder with me so I can climb to the top of that pole you have waiting for me, lol.' She also mentioned that she would be ten minutes later than planned.

On her arrival, Tony noticed that she had dyed her hair a golden blonde and had curled it; she wore a long, black dress with an open back, clearly revealing that she wasn't wearing a bra. The front of the dress showed an encouraging amount of cleavage, which she was very keen to push towards Tony as he greeted her. They descended the twenty-one steps that led to the basement apartment, while

Eszter told him more about the robbery at the Saunders'. As they got to the bottom of the stairwell, she admitted that her brother-in-law had gone crazy when he found out they'd been robbed.

After their first bottle of wine, she jokingly said, 'When my brother-in-law said that the well was robbed, I thought it might have been you, ha ha.' She then became very serious, and lowering her tone, said, 'But after they found the dogs' shallow graves, we were astonished – it was so savage, the way the dogs were killed. I thought that you wouldn't have been able to do something as bad as that.'

Tony felt no need to respond, so he just shook his head. When she finished telling the tale, he opened the second bottle of expensive white wine, noticing in the half-light that Eszter seemed to be more attractive all of a sudden.

Tony placed his empty glass on the coffee table and leaned towards her. He pulled her head towards him and she leaned in for an embrace. Her tongue entered his mouth, hungrily searching for his. Her heart was pounding against his chest. He kissed her face, then her neck, slowly moving down to her chest. She gasped as he moved lower, then lower still, and she lifted the skirt of her dress, instinctively. She laid back and closed her eyes as Tony gave her more pleasure in ten minutes than she had experienced in the last ten months. When she had climaxed and he finally emerged, she kissed him deeply and gratefully. He moved on top of her slipping inside her with ease, slowly taking them both to an even more intense climax. Once they were both spent, they got dressed and Tony walked to the gate with Eszter, bidding her farewell. The apartment was a mess and it needed to be tidied. 'That can wait until tomorrow,' Tony said to himself. He had used the last of his energy on his lover, so instead, he flopped back down on the sofa and fell into a deep, fulfilled sleep.

CHAPTER THREE

Nicky and Tony messaged each other reiterating that they were in the clear; they were clearly elated about their fortune. They decided to throw a riverside party with some of their acquaintances with a view to showing off a little of their wealth. They needed to entice Daniel Martin and an acquaintance called Thaddeus to join their next undertaking. Who's Thaddeus, you might ask? Well … he's an ex-convict who has spent a considerable amount of time in an maximum security prison for multiple murders and armed robberies. Useful, but dangerous.

He was released from prison a few years ago, with plenty of knowledge and a wealth of criminal networks, human resources at his fingertips and Mr Chin. On meeting Thaddeus, people instantly understood that he wasn't someone to rag with. A little over two metres tall, he was burly and emitted an unmistakable odour of a decaying corpse as if he had been submerged in embalming fluid. He never smiled and the sclera of his eyes were crimson red, as though someone had filled them in with a thick blunt red pen. There was something unreal about him; he was like Lucifer in the flesh. Many people said that he dabbled in witchcraft; either way, he wasn't to be taken lightly.

Nicky and Tony discussed their previous casual meetings with the character. They knew he could obtain the supply of counterfeit bank notes they needed to complete their plan. Marianna would supply the cash bags, money seals, and other banking stock. During their first encounter with the 'Lucifer', the deal was that he got them a few thousand bank notes. When the job was finished, he was greedy and overcharged them with demands for fifty percent of their takings. Back then, they were quite naïve, but this time they were wiser and ready to demand a better outcome.

Mr Chin's printing press operated on a busy main street. He carried out legitimate work, printing brochures and promoting items for many companies, including banks. However, behind the scenes, the company was the hub of the underworld's best manufacturer of counterfeit notes, bank drafts, and traveller cheques. You name it, he produced it. Whatever print was required, Mr Chin always delivered at the right price, but he was so inundated with orders from various dealers, no-one was allowed to talk to him directly. The only way to contact Mr Chin was through Lucifer, well … Thaddeus. An order as large as theirs would take him several months to produce, but they knew the notes would look authentic.

Tony and Nicky needed this deal to go through glitch free and for the recipients at the bank vault to only realise months later that the money was fake. It would take considerable time to figure out what had happened and how, and, by then, everyone involved would have had time to disassociate themselves from each other and the heist, or at least be in hiding. It was time to set their plans in motion. They sent invites to twenty of their friends including Erika, Linzi, Inga, Stella, Ioannis, Marc, Ioanna, Sofia, Lexi, Isabella, Laszlo, and Stephanie. They had to make an impression, so, for the sake of their freedom to bed the other women, Marianna wasn't allowed to attend. They needed the right mix of gorgeous and flirtatious gals and boys with sports cars that showed power and wealth.

Thaddeus wasn't a stranger to that lifestyle either. After finishing his various sentences, he had invested time and money in two strip clubs, one located in Spanish Green and the other in Bramshill. It's often said that you shouldn't mix business with pleasure, but being the sort of person he is, Thaddeus was oblivious to such theories. On many occasions he had sex with the ladies who worked at the clubs. Very often, and without caring, he took them back to the house he shared with his partner, Marlena and their one-year-old child, Richard. Marlena's objection to this elicit behaviour would meet the back of his hand or a clenched fist. His abuse was relentless, but as Marlena didn't have any other means of supporting herself or her child, she had to tolerate him and pay the consequence.

Nicky and Tony agreed that the abandoned old barn, four hundred yards west of Weatherpool, which had stood desolate and reportedly haunted, would be the perfect spot for their gathering. The old barn, nicknamed 'The Spots', had its own untold stories, with ramshackle tractors, upturned rusty rims, and bales of hay dotted around the landscape. It was as if the owners had left suddenly. Some parts of the hay had stains; many say they were from dried blood, which echoed the claim that the building was haunted. The backdrop to the barn comprised of disease-riddled cedar, pine, sycamore, willow, juniper and dried ferns, making it look and feel like autumn all year round. The spot was a perfect place for invitees to indulge themselves in a little illicit behaviour as not many people were brave enough to venture there.

'What's on the menu?' Tony asked.

'The menu??' Nicky swatted. 'Bitches, booze, and whatever nibbles they can get at the grill takeaway at the end of my street, I would say!'

'I'll drive the pickup truck and you can drive my motorbike!' said Nicky, in an assuring voice as he walked towards the door. They set off for supplies for the event; they decided on some checkered tablecloths so they could use the bales of hay as tables. They bought an Igloo cooler with ice and plenty to drink – after all, a party would not be a party without Hennessy cognac, tequila, and vodka.

That afternoon, they were the first to arrive at the venue. The barn was as eerie as ever, but it was the right place to set the mood. Tony messaged Daniel to see if he was still attending. He replied with an emphatic 'yes'.

After setting out their goods, Nicky and Tony quenched their thirst with an ice-cold lager. The cold crisp taste was so good. Ten minutes later, and on their second lager, they saw a male figure approaching on the footpath.

'That looks like Daniel, Nicky', said Tony, slurping the frothy head from the top of his glass. 'Actually, it looks like they're all arriving now ... look!'

Behind him, they could see a red M3 series BMW, which would be Marc's. An entourage of vehicles followed, all high-end and high-spec vehicles, some of which Tony and Nicky didn't recognise until their occupants climbed out. They approached the vehicles as they pulled up in a neat, well-organised line. Thaddeus introduced Nicky and Tony to his friend, Kwame, and said that they had a lot to talk about. He told them that Kwame was in the West African diamond trade. He said that the problem he had was that he didn't know anyone that would be willing to buy uncertified diamonds. Thaddeus explained that the diamonds they had were all mined legally but were not Kimberly Process Certified, making it illegal to trade them outside Africa. He went onto say that although they had a solid system for bringing them in to Europe, no one was interested in buying them.

Nicky and Tony knew a few people in the diamond smuggling district, which was a stone's throw away from Chancery Lane tube station; these people would buy diamonds with or without a certificate. Many believe that the Kimberley Certificate is only designed to keep African countries poor. How can the same diamond without a certificate be worth five hundred dollars and after certification, be worth five million?

By now their party was in full swing, and everyone was in high spirits; those with a common interest were huddled together in small groups. Nicky, Thaddeus, Kwame, Daniel, and Tony drifted from the from the barn and sat on a bale of hay under the dying willow tree. They discussed how the diamond business could work. It was clear from the onset that Thaddeus wanted to take control. He insisted that he would get forty percent of any money made from the import and sale of the diamonds.

'All right, lets agree to that', said Nicky, sarcastically. 'So, Thaddeus, yours and Kwame's job is to get the diamonds out of West Africa and to Weatherpool?!'

'Ras clath', replied Thaddeus, speaking in an inappropriate Jamaican slang, which translated as 'fuck off'.

Nicky shrugged his shoulders and looked at Tony. 'I don't like dealing with stupid people. If they can't agree with our terms, this diamond business will have to be put back on the shelf.'

Thaddeus sprung up from the bale he was sitting on. The two-metre figure stood over the friends and his shadow towered upwards into the willow branches. Before, they could blink, Thaddeus had pulled out a black nine millimetre Glock.

'Shit!' Tony shouted, jumping to his feet. Everyone's reactions were different: some ducked, some hid, but they were all staring at the Lucifer-like figure.

'Are you calling me stupid?!?' he muttered, staring at Nicky, who was standing behind the bale of hay that they had been sitting on.

'Hey! Let's calm things down a bit!' shouted Kwame. 'Are we here to have a good time and make some money, or what?' He continued, 'It's a nice day and I'll tell you what ... I've been looking at some of that ass over there and I need to get laid before I leave this party. So why don't we relax and use the other guns that God gave us?!'

They all broke out into laughter. 'I second that!' said Tony as he moved towards Nicky.

Kwame chuckled and said, 'Come on, let's talk

about this later...' He nodded at Thaddeus, who, reluctantly nodded back and returned his Glock to its holster.

They dispersed from the group and started to mingle with other guests, especially some of the girls who accompanied Thaddeus. They knew that the girls that Thaddeus has brought with him were all prostitutes and were under his control, but they were stunning – the complete opposite of Eszter.

'Hey bro! Tony snapped at Nicky. 'What the fuck was that all about!'

Nicky groaned and muttered under his breath, 'If you play with the devil, don't be surprise if you get burned.'

'I understand ... I do ... I know what you mean!' Tony sighed. 'But let's at least have some fun! This party was our idea!'

Looking at Nicky, Tony muttered, 'I don't think Lucifer understands that he's fucking with the wrong angels'. Nicky nodded his head slightly in agreement.

They continued walking over to where a group

of their female invitees were sitting on a derelict tractor, joining in with their conversation, which was about different types of technology and how it was difficult to avoid the changes that are taking place throughout the world. Their conversation drifted on to clothes and, typically, ended with a conversation about sex. One thing led to another and before they knew it, Nicky and Stephanie were kissing. It wasn't the first time those two set of lips had wrestled. That was one of reasons that Marianna hadn't been invited to this gathering. She would probably have pulled out a gun too.

Nicky led his mistress by the hand to a space in the barn, behind the bales and away from the others. He looked over at Tony, and put his finger to his lips in a kind of 'Keep it shut' expression. Gradually, all of the other party members paired up in various parts of the barn (some in three's or more) and expressions of lust echoed through the rafters.

When everyone was spent, the party began disperse. It had been somewhat successful; the two men had achieved their main objectives and Tony was very clear where they all stood in terms of future events. Thaddeus was the first to get in his car, taking his guests with him. Nicky and Tony began to clear away the empty bottles and other rubbish that had been strewn around the barn. No one would care if they left it messy, but that was how they operated. They always cleaned up forensically after themselves. Just before they set off home, Nicky and Tony agreed to arrange another meeting with Thaddeus, so they could get things back on track.

Nicky told Tony to set off on the 600cc motorbike ahead of him and said he would follow in his 4X4 pickup truck. It was only after Tony had sat on the motorbike that he realised that he'd had a lot to drink. He couldn't feel the helmet as he put it on his head and the bike felt a lot lighter than usual. It was as though he had gained superhuman strength. He hesitated.

Nicky drove up beside him and asked, 'Are you ok, Teach?'

'Yeah, I'm fine!' Tony coughed. 'It's just strange that your bike doesn't feel as heavy as before, that's all!'

'Ok ...' Nicky replied, looking at Tony strangely. 'Can we get going then??'

'Yeah mate, I'm ready' Tony answered, shaking his head a little.

He started the bike's engine and revved it . He shook his head again. He revved it again then moved off. The motorbike did feel lighter ... and faster. Before he knew it, he was doing sixty miles per hour. Tony could see Nicky's truck headlights fading in the distance behind him. He caught up with two cars that had set off ahead of him, but instead of slowing down, Tony increased his speed to eighty miles per hour, and overtook them. It was like they were standing still as he flashed past them.

There was another set of vehicles ahead. It was getting darker and had started raining, so visibility was getting worse. Tony could sense this but the bike felt so light, he defiantly lifted the front wheel and overtook the next four vehicles, but as he set the front wheel down onto the asphalt to negotiate the approaching corner, the back wheel skidded. The front wheel did a dance, left, then right, then threw Tony up and over the front of the bike.

The helmet-protected his head, as he hit the ground hard and the asphalt ripped through his Moschino jeans and blue Hugo Boss shirt, cruelly slicing off the skin beneath. Pebbles and grit were embedded in his raw skin. The pain was intense for a moment, then it was dulled as a dazzling light took his attention. He felt like he was being lifted and carried through the white brightness. He floated for a second and then everything when black.

Tony woke up to the sound of a woman crying. Her voice and smell were familiar, but he didn't recognised the soft hand that was stroking his forehead. He opened his eyes to a brightly lit room and an intense headache. Even though his vision was blurred, he recognised Marianna, whose tearful voice and gentle touch had woken him. Tony tried to speak but he realised that his jaw was immobilised with a bandage that enveloped his entire head. His legs also felt slightly bizarre. He could feel them but they wouldn't move they felt like a dead weight.

Tony's lips moved as he tried to ask Marianna what had happened. 'Where's Nicky?' he tried to say. He was so confused ... had he been shot? Had Nicky been shot? Was he alive? The last thing he remembered was Thaddeus standing there pointing a gun at his friend. He had so many questions. He saw a doctor approaching, who stood behind Marianna and said, 'You're extremely lucky to be alive. You've been in accident and have been unconscious for the past eight hours; please don't try to move or talk. I'll fill you in on the details later. You're in a good place now. No broken bones, so no surgery necessary. Get some rest and we'll see how you are tomorrow.'

Marianna's sobbing faded as she continue to stroke Tony's forehead. His arm was tight. It felt like it was being pulled by something metal and sharp. The skin on his forearm was totally gone, replaced by a sheet of dry blood. At the time, he didn't know that his right leg and back were in the same state. He tried to ease forward to see his injuries, but there was no chance of that happening; the blood on his back was stuck to the bedding. It was then that he realised the extent of his injuries. He was going to be hospital bound for some time.

The days turned into weeks. Since the accident, Tony had made new friends, met many people, and began to realise that he was respected by more than he realised, including the hundreds of students that he'd taught over the years. Along with the daily visits from Marianna, he also had a twice-daily visit from Tamara, a past student, who Tony hadn't realised was so fond of him. Tamara would be at his bedside even before Marianna arrived and she would be the last person he saw every evening.

His time in hospital also gave Tony time to think about everything that had happened as well as about his and Nicky's ongoing projects. He knew Nicky was angry because he had told Marianna that he should have been more careful. It turned out that Nicky had also had an accident on that same night. Marianna told Tony that Nicky arrived at the scene of his accident a minute or so after it had happened. He was so worried that it would take too long for an ambulance to arrive, he put him into the back of his pickup truck. In his rush to get to the hospital, Nicky failed to negotiate a corner and crashed into a utility pool. It was fortunate that a past student recognised that Tony was unconscious and bleeding and rushed him to hospital in his car.

So that day had ended far worse that anyone had expected; not only had Thaddeus pulled a gun on them, but they both could have died in accidents. Thinking this through, all of a sudden, Tony understood why Nicky had not visited him in hospital – he was angry.

Six weeks had passed and the doctors overseeing his treatment felt that Tony had made sufficient progress and were comfortable with him going home to complete his recovery. His natural skin had started to grow over his wounds, replacing the painful shredded layers. Although his skin was tight and he ached constantly, Tony felt much stronger and he could walk unaided. Although his head injuries were not life threatening or life changing, he felt a constant pain in his chin and jaw that would continue to remind him of the accident. The doctors reminded him that being physically fit before the accident had saved him. It had reduced the severity of his injuries and aided his recovery.

Tony was grateful for being able to finally go home. However, he wasn't well enough to go back to his teaching job. Marianna had told him that Nicky was busy carrying on with the work that he and Tony had started. She also said that he didn't visit me in hospital because he didn't want to talk about what he was doing. Marianna mentioned that Nicky would pick him up from the hospital and take him home. Tony hoped that would give them the opportunity to wipe the slate clean and catch up with the recent events he had missed.

At approximately two-thirty pm, the doctor told Tony that he was being discharged. He smiled, sat up on the bed, and reached out his hand to show his appreciation for the care that the doctors had provided during the past six weeks. As the doctor left the room, Tony sighed, not sure what to expect from Nicky. There was just one thing for certain, Tony had missed out on a lot and would need to get back in shape pretty quickly.

Tony got up, dressed himself and packed his things. The clock on the wall showed two-forty-five, roughly the time that Marianna had told him that Nicky would be at the hospital entrance to pick him up. Tony opened the closed curtains, picked up his holdall, and walked out of the ward to the passageway that led to the reception area and exit. As Tony left, he had said goodbye to other patient and nurses; they had become an intimate part of his life (some knew his body better than his own mother).

The exit led to a red no parking zone, so only emergency vehicles were allowed to park there. A huge oak tree stood twenty metres away from the entrance to the hospital's garden. In front of it stood a taxi and a silver and black AMG M-class Mercedes. Tony looked around, but couldn't see any sign of Nicky. Suddenly, the driver's door of the Mercedes opened and Nicky alighted, shouting 'Teach … I'm here!'

Tony was delighted to see his best friend after such a long time. Nicky rushed over and hugged him with his right arm, whilst relieving him of his bag with his left. 'Come on … Let's go! We have a lot of catching up to do!' Nicky sighed as they walked together to the four-by-four vehicle and held onto Tony's right shoulder as they stopped at the passenger side of the Mercedes.

They paused and Nicky looked at him seriously then said, 'Promise me you won't do something as crazy as that again!' He exhaled a deep breath and continued, 'I blame myself for what happened to you; I shouldn't have allowed you to drive the motorbike after what you'd had to drink. I've made a promise to myself to look after you better in the future!' He sighed as if a great load had lifted from his shoulders.

Tony welled up with emotion. 'Brother, it was my fault. I should have been more careful!' His voice croaked ... 'Thanks for looking out for me ... you're a true friend!'

It was all getting too emotional, so Tony shifted the conversation.

'Hey, you've been up to a lot it seems!' As Tony pointed to the Mercedes. 'Is this ride yours?'

Nicky looked at the menacing black and chrome eighteen inch rims, before turning his head back to look at Tony. 'It's not mine, Teach – it's actually OURS!'

'After the accident, I decided we should change our image and we had the money to do just that' he continued.

Tony's eyes widened in delight. 'Wow, that's amazing ... and thoughtful! Especially considering that it's my fault that you now don't have a motorbike or truck.' He bowed his head shamefully.

Nicky laughed, 'Oh, that's all behind us now. We have a lot of money to make and loads to catch up on. How about we get something to eat … at our usual place?'

After six weeks of a controlled diet in hospital, eating a restaurant meal was certainly appealing but the afternoon sunshine and the smells emanating from the polluted air mixed with the fragrance of the hospital gardens that rushed to Tony's head. He suddenly felt nauseous and dizzy. Noticing him wobbling on his feet, Nicky grabbed the door handle and pulled it open. Tony slumped headfirst onto the tan leather. Nicky quickly sat in the driver's seat and pulled Tony upright the best he could.

'Hey! Are you all right?' he asked, giving Tony a shake to make sure he was still conscious.

With closed eyes, Tony nodded. 'Yeah, I'm just feeling a bit dizzy, but I'll be ok.' He held onto the inner door handle and pushed himself upright. With every breath Tony could smell petrol; Tony inhaled as much as he could. He felt like a substance abuser; it seemed to boost his vision and, all of a sudden, he didn't feel dizzy anymore. He propped himself up on the passenger seat, looking through the windscreen and onto the car's bonnet.

'I can see what you mean about using your imagination!' Tony paused, taking in a deep breath. 'This ride definitely makes more than one statement. It must've cost a lot?'

Nicky looked at Tony and smiled, 'Teach … you don't have to worry. I haven't blown all our money.' His smile turned into laughter, 'Come on, let's get something to eat and I will update you on everything I've been up to.'

The turbo engine roared as the in-vehicle music system came on. Tony could feel the power as they pulled out from the hospital driveway onto the street. He attempted an excited 'Whoop whoop!!' but instantly regretted it, clutching his side in pain.

CHAPTER FOUR

They arrived at the restaurant having not had much of an opportunity to talk properly because of all the fun they'd had in the car. They alighted from their vehicle and Nicky started to walk away. Tony called, 'Hang on mate … I can't move that fast.' Nicky stepped back and helped Tony out of the passenger seat. There was a prominent smell of petrol coming from the petrol station adjoining the restaurant car park. Tony's body reacted to the stench like it would to an amphetamine, giving him a much needed boost. He stepped forward and gingerly walked towards the restaurant's entrance. The familiar employees looked on with curiosity as Tony walked through the restaurant like an inebriated sailor on the deck of a sailboat during a storm.

They made their way to their favourite table and the waiter courteously pulled a chair out for Tony. 'Thanks!' he sighed, dropping his backside onto the wooden chair like a sack of potatoes.

Tony looked at Nicky, who was already seated. He hadn't realised how sore he was going to feel. He knew that he should really still be in hospital recovering.

'What are you having, Teach?' Nicky's voice echoed in the empty enclave of the restaurant.

'I'm not sure, but I definitely want soup!' He browsed through the triangular shaped menu. 'Tum yum soup, followed by duck in black bean sauce and a portion of Singapore noodles. How about you, brother?' he asked.

Nicky's eyebrows knitted as he replied, 'Hmm … I'm feeling a little adventurous … I'm having deep fried frog legs in black-bean sauce with mixed vegetable fried rice … and we need two glasses of Chinese beer to wet our pallets.' He licked his lips and returned the menu to the centre of the table, beckoning the waiter.

The waiter took the order and as he left, Nicky said 'I need to update you on everything that's happened in the last six weeks … there's a lot to tell you. Where should I start?!'

He paused, then began …

'In your absence, I had to seek the assistance of my Uncle Darren … you remember him? He's the mechanic with the garage in Free Port. The garage that has the apple trees that we used to climb after school?!'

'Oh yeah! replied Tony. He's a serious player!' Tony paused while he caught his breath then continued. 'What level of assistance are we talking about?'

'Well!' Nicky replied in a hushed tone. 'You

remember he spent time in prison for multiple homicide?'

'Yeah, a long time ago …' Tony rebutted.

'Exactly! Well, it turns out he served time in prison with Thaddeus!'

'Wow … small world, and even smaller in prison!' Tony replied.

'Uncle Darren is more resourceful than you can imagine. He has given me an insight into the way Thaddeus works and a lot more! For starters, he told me that Thaddeus won't allow us to walk away from this deal alive!'

'What?!' Tony exclaimed. 'What do you mean by that!?'

'Well, Uncle Darren told me that half of the murders committed by Thaddeus were direct results of business deals. Apparently, Thaddeus always covers his tracks! We need to be very careful of him and this deal! That's one of the reasons we need my uncle,' he whispered as the waiter returned to the table with their meals.

Puzzled and suddenly petrified, Tony wondered where this left them. As the waiter left the table, he hissed 'Are you serious?'

'Yeah..!' Nicky replied. 'Uncle Darren knows even more than he's told me but he said he will help us ... he knows exactly how this will turn out, and, I'm telling you now, it won't be in our favour.'

Nicky reached for his glass of beer. Even though Tony's beer was sitting temptingly in front of him, he didn't move. He felt pale and had frozen to the spot. Nicky noticed this and stared at him from across the table.

'Teach ... don't worry! We have this covered. I will explain everything in detail. But before we make any more moves you need to get back up to strength and be ready to face what's ahead.'

He went on to say that he and Marianna had organised a physiotherapist, personal fitness instructor, and a nutritionist, alongside acupuncture and massage sessions for him to support his recovery. Nick outlined an uncomfortable scenario that would see them continuing on a dangerous path of new personal discoveries. Adding to their plans to heist the twenty three million, they would smuggle a huge wealth of diamonds from West and Central Africa.

Nicky explained that Thaddeus' friend, Kwame, was well connected. He had friends in the Zimbabwe, Democratic Republic of the Congo, Angola and Ghana governments. He would arrange for them to collect visas from those countries' embassies but that it was up to the two friends to travel there and meet with the various groups. Nicky explained that he had also met with Mr Sheikh, their contact in the diamond district near Chancery Lane station and that they were ready to go whenever they were. Nicky's uncle's garage would be the nucleus of the operation; in there already was the first delivery of counterfeit money, money bags, and wraps.

Nicky finished his explanation by saying, 'You need to focus on your recovery, Teach; in three weeks' time, we're flying to Africa to get the ball rolling.'

The two men left the restaurant after four and half hours; the sun was now dipping behind the hilltop. As they made their way to their vehicle, Tony reflected on everything that Nicky had told him. The details of the heist seemed pretty straightforward, even though there were many complex issues to overcome before the actual event. Nonetheless, with Nicky's Uncle Darren involved, things would be much easier than they would be otherwise. Tony's science background would also be extremely useful.

After a twenty-five minute drive, they arrived in Weatherpool. Nicky carried Tony's bag to the side entrance and bid him farewell with a brotherly handshake. Tony took a deep breath and continued through the yard and into the kitchen, where his brother, Everton, was busy preparing sandwiches.

'I wasn't expecting you home today!' Everton exclaimed. 'I thought the doc said you were being discharged tomorrow?'

Tony replied, 'Yeah, but when they examined me this morning, they decided I was fit to be discharged. No more treatment needed, apparently. I left the hospital a while ago, but needed to reacquaint myself with some Chinese cuisine and catch up with Nicky. You know how it is when we get talking.'

'Ok, well, you can stay in my basement apartment, so you get more privacy. You'll need it while you're recovering.'

Wrapping his sandwiches in kitchen foil, he continued, 'Mum and dad are in Miami for the next six months, so we have the place to ourselves. I won't be here much!'

After zipping up his rucksack, he stepped forward and patted Tony on the shoulder. 'It's wonderful to have you home, Tony. But PLEASE don't do something that stupid again.'

Tony replied, 'Thanks', and watched his brother dart out of the side door. It seemed that everyone was blaming his accident on reckless driving. He realised they were right to do so. 'I'm an idiot', he muttered to himself, switching the kettle on for a desperately needed cup of coffee.

One of the benefits of being a teacher is the school holidays and there are none better than the summer break. During this time, educators can let their hair down and relax. For a few weeks, there are no lesson plans to complete and there's no marking to do. For Tony, the summer holiday was due to start in three weeks, but being on sick leave, he wouldn't be in work until September. He hoped that he wouldn't need to go back to teaching at all.

The conversation Nicky and Tony had in the restaurant still lingered in his head. Smuggling diamonds was a different league to anything else they had done. Diamonds, naturally created from carbon during volcanic activity, are one of the most beautiful things in the world. But ... getting the stones in the first place would be problematic. They would then have to transfer the diamonds from West Africa and sell them at an agreed price. In their pure or natural state, diamonds are rough, dirty, and less valuable. Their value increases once they are processed: cut, polished, and Kimberley certified. The Kimberley certification claims to prevent conflict diamonds (also known as blood diamonds) from entering the mainstream flow of legitimate diamonds. But how do you define a diamond that is or isn't conflict free? Who decides that a somewhat worthless stone becomes an item that is worth dying for? A stone that has a start value of fifty dollars to a local African miner, could go through a corrupt system and eventually be revalued at five hundred thousand or even five million when it's processed in Europe. With that said, greed is the most brutal sacrifice of all ... Nicky told Tony at the restaurant that Thaddeus, alias Lucifer, had demanded fifty percent of all deals for himself. That meant he would walk away with approximately eleven million from the Brinks heist and half of whatever money they made from the diamonds. In return, he would provide the means for them to get the diamonds out of Africa and onto the continent. Likewise for the heist, together with Daniel Martin, who was now under Thaddeus' physical and mental control, and Darren, Nicky's uncle, who was at the centre of the whole project, he would provide a network of individuals who work for the Brinks company to see it through to a successful end.

Tony decided to meet up with Kwame at a pub to discuss the start of their next multimillion dollar project. They needed to put their simple ideas and instructions into motion.

It was 7:30pm on a pleasant summers day when he arrived at the venue, The Spotted Arms. He pushed the heavy green door open and walked straight into a dingy and drab room with a grotty, sticky, un-vacuumed carpet and old stained wallpaper. The bar was untidy, with used glasses, small puddles of liquid, and crumbs spilling out from snack packets. There was also a musty smell lingering in the air, probably from the filthy carpets and upholstery. The number of people drinking outside gave the false impression that the bar was packed inside. It was surprisingly quiet – probably because the crowd preferred the fresh air.

Tony looked around for a suitable and clean enough space to sit. A place where likeminded people could engage in a frank discussion about making millions.

There were three tables in the corner away from the toilets. This would mean less footfall from other customers. There, they would be able to talk privately and discuss their diamond trafficking project. Tony approached the bar, ordered himself a Corona with lime, and then made his way over to a table on the right. As he sat down, he took notice of the few patrons that were seated at the other tables. They all seemed too engrossed in their own affairs to care about anyone else. Before long, he had halved his drink, but Kwame was still nowhere to be seen.

'I hope he hasn't changed his mind', Tony said to himself. Suddenly, three black men walked into the bar; Kwame walked in last at the back of the entourage. Tony raised his hand to get his attention. He acknowledged the gesture and all three men came to Tony's table.

Tony stood up and greeted the men with 'Good evening!' He stretched his hand towards Kwame, who reciprocated the handshake and went on to introduce the two other men. The shorter of the two, Mario, was Angolan and the other, was Seidu, a Ghanaian. As with most first meetings, there was a somewhat tense atmosphere.

'What are you drinking, guys? Tony asked. He smiled and moved his chair back and out of the way so he could squeeze past the men and get to the bar.

All three men opted for stronger drinks, befitting of their African masculinity: double whiskeys. Costly, but worth it. As Tony returned from the bar, he could see that the men had relaxed a little and were chatting about a girl that they had bumped into on the train on their way to this meeting. The tone of their conversation suggested that all three were very close friends.

Tony placed the tray with the drinks order on the table , picked up his own, and said 'Help yourselves guys. Three double Hennessy whiskeys as requested!' It took them a few minutes to reach for their glasses as they continued with their chatter about the woman and then about Range Rovers. It was clear that the reason for our meeting wasn't to make money to secure a better life for their families. It was about enjoying all that life had to offer at that moment, including women and fast cars. In a way, Tony wasn't impressed with this, but he knew that, sometimes, it was necessary to take a taste of something sour before you can taste something sweet.

Tony interjected by asking Kwame if he'd seen the current price of gold. Kwame responded with 'Yes! It's now thirty two thousand dollars per kilo.' He paused to sip his drink, then added, 'Right now, I'd be happy with four kilos.'

Kwame and Seidu talked more about Ghana and where the gold could be found. They said that, even though the government there was cracking down on illegal and small-scale mining, there were many ways that we could get into the business without too much investment or risk. The key was to buy land and set up a small mining operation. For a successful start-up they would need seven thousand dollars for the land and equipment and the right people on the ground to manage the mine, known locally as galamsey. They discussed how it would all work on the ground in Ghana. The guys all agreed that a town called Obausi was the best place to set up the ops, because they knew a lot of people at a local level and it was in a central location to the other mining communities. First they would need to visit the location to assess the practicalities, such as how were they were going to take the gold out of Ghana and to the Europe. There were obstacles to overcome, so the sooner they got started, the quicker they would start reaping the benefits.

The conversation between the men went on for at least three hours, during which time they had consumed enough alcohol to relax the conversation, which now flowed with ease. As the conversation became more in-depth and creative, Mario mentioned that he had a few contacts in Angola who could provide them with diamonds. Interestingly, he hinted that his contacts were ex-military or current government ministers. It was now up to the men to agree on a credible plan that would allow them to successfully take on the diamond project AND the heist. They decided to part company for now and consider their resources. They were just about to stand up and shake hands when, all of a sudden, they heard the crash of a glass bottle and shouting from outside the pub. Kwame, in true security guard fashion, said, 'Come on, let's get out this way; we can't risk the police seeing us as a group'. He turned and led the group through the rear door of the pub. As they left, a woman screamed and a man shouted, 'Oh fuck … he's been stabbed. Call an ambulance!!!'

As the men walked across the rear car park and away down the street, they could hear the chaos and confusion of people trying to make sense of what had just happened. Looking back, Tony saw a white male on the ground in a pool of blood. Bystanders were starting to circle the man as Kwame and his group casually walked away from the scene. They made their way to the train station to contemplate their future projects.

On his way home, Tony thought about everything that needed to be done. With the summer holidays only being six weeks long, there wasn't much time for him and Nicky to work together to get things moving, especially with the Brinks heist on the cards too. Tony got onto a train that would take him to the Weatherpool's neighbouring town Spanish Green. From there, it would take him 15 minutes to walk home, giving him enough time to collect his thoughts and call his trusted buddy to get an update on how things were going. When he stepped off the train, he called Nicky's Skype ID ... it rang for about 30 seconds. On the second attempt, it rang for a full minute. It was unusual for Nicky not to pick up a call. Tony waited for ten minutes and called him again. This time, he picked up after 15 seconds.

'You ok bro?' Tony asked.

'Yeah!' He replied in a low voice. 'I was in the middle of sorting out a situation, but all is good, don't worry.' From the sound of Nicky's voice, Tony thought that it didn't sound like things were good at all. He pressed Nicky. 'Are you sure everything is OK bro?'

Nicky took a few second to answer. At this point, Tony knew for sure there was a problem. Nicky admitted, 'We need to pay Mr Chin more money to complete his task and Lucifer is asking for five hundred dollars to buys some things.'

'Tony repeated, 'We need to pay Mr Chin more money?' He paused and a long silence followed.

'Nicky, are you still there?' Tony asked, listening to Nicky's faint breathing.

'Yeah, I'm ok ...' he stuttered. 'I just don't know about this deal ... people are getting greedy.'

'What do you mean?' replied Tony. 'Some of the guys on the truck are saying that their cut at the moment isn't enough. We all know why the cash supply is short, but what can we do about it?'

Nicky replied, 'We know what the "problem" is and it would be a case of getting rid of it after the deal has gone through.'

For now, they could only continue working through the process of getting things ready. Nicky mentioned that, along with asking for more money, the Brinks gang wanted to speed up the process. This was because they often needed to move to different areas for their business, which meant that the company had no stable teams. There was a sensible system of moving people around so that no close relationships were formed amongst the staff.

Nicky and Tony were already in too deep to pull out, so they would just have to carry on and figure out how they were going to get it all to work in their best interests. Their conversation ended with many unanswered questions but they knew that they had to make sure they stayed alive long enough to enjoy the fruits of their labour.

CHAPTER FIVE

On his way home, Tony thought through all the systems that they would have to build to transport the diamonds from Kinboasi, West Africa to Europe. It wasn't going to be easy task on many levels.

As he dodged countless road renovations and newly constructed buildings in Spanish Green, he considered the barriers they had to overcome, including getting visas and travelling to the remote mining regions of Kinboasi. They needed a first-hand account of the proposed work ahead, the cultures of the area, and the logistics of transporting the diamonds. After 20 minutes of playing 'dodge the scaffolding', he arrived at the automatic gate at the entrance of his driveway, knocked back another Hennessey whisky, and, without any further consideration, went straight to bed.

From the discussion in the bar, Kwame needed seven thousand five hundred dollars in cash to secure their visas and international medical documents to travel to West Africa. They agreed they would provide everything that he required within five days, after which, they could book their flights. The two friends decided that Tony would focus on the diamonds business while Nicky would concentrate on getting the Brink's heist underway, mainly because he had direct contact with the people involved.

As a precaution, Kwame insisted that they should travel on separate fights; however, if that wasn't possible, they would at the very least have to sit away from each other with no contact. Tony didn't really understand why this was necessary. What was the point in hiding from each other and being so secretive if the proposed business was legitimate. Tony humoured him though, and as instructed, booked a separate flight. Kwame was keen that Tony's flight should arrive at their destination during the evening and he would do the same. Kwame provided a general description of the airport in Sanibo, West Africa and told Tony to wait in a Chinese restaurant that was on the right of the airport's exit.

After nearly six hours in the air, the first officer announced that the plane was starting to descend and would be landing shortly. The temperature forecast was a sunny twenty eight degrees Celsius. From the air, it was easy to see the difference between this landscape and that of Europe or United States. There was an absence of high-rise congested building developments and, instead, the terrain was blanketed with bright red clay-like soil, which could be seen between the greenery in the canopy of tall trees. Rooftops of various colours and shapes intermingled with patches of parched land on which wildlife could be seen grazing and, far below the plane, birds flew. Sanibo seemed to be part wilderness, part city, as if it had been half developed then abandoned.

As Tony disembarked the KLM plane into the

familiar setting of an arrival lounge. He noticed that whilst the outside of the building seemed fairly modern, the arrival lounge was simplistic. There were no screens displaying arriving flights or terminals. There were very few lights; the ceilings were low and dark-coloured walls made the huge room even more dreary. The queue of all two hundred and forty passengers stretched from the immigration counter to the entrance door. The lounge had as many staff as passengers.

As he moved closer to the immigration counter, an officer asked everyone in the queue to have their yellow international medical book available. Tony's heart sank at this, as Kwame hadn't given him such a thing. He tried to think back to when Kwame gave him his paperwork, but surely he would remember a yellow medical book.

As Tony took couple of steps closer to the immigration desk, his head still bowed, trying to work out a strategy, a coarse voice pelted 'Can I see your travel documents and your yellow international medical book?'

Tony lifted his head when he realised the

immigration officer was speaking to him.

'Are you talking to me?' he checked.

'Yes, you ... I wasn't talking to myself!' the immigration officer smirked and looked at one of his colleagues, a security guard, who was brandishing a holstered pistol. Tony nodded and rummaged through his holdall side pocket to find his passport and the yellow book.

'Here you go, Sir,' Tony politely replied, handing over what he thought the man needed.

'Ha, ha, ha!' The officer laughed as he took his passport and the thin yellow pamphlet that Kwame had given to Tony. He looked through Tony's passport and checked the visa date. He then picked up the yellow pamphlet and looked over the top of his glasses at Tony, with a smirk on his face.

'And what is this?' The officer's grin turned into a menacing frown.

'Well', Tony stuttered. 'I was given that pamphlet to bring with me ... I thought this was all I needed!'

The immigration officer beckoned to the security guard then turned back to Tony, grunting, 'You need to come with us'. The immigration officer and security guard exchanged a few words in a language that Tony couldn't fathom.

'Why? I don't understand!' Tony choked. It was clear to him that he had been set up, but it didn't make sense. Why would Kwame give him the pamphlet when he knew that they would ask for an official medical book?! The security guard instructed Tony to step out of the queue and then escorted him to a door just to the right of the lounge. The immigration officer entered first, then Tony was ushered in, followed by the security guard, who was resting his hand on his pistol, as if he thought he was going to need to use it.

As he entered the room, Tony's heart sank. 'What have I got myself into now?' he thought. 'I don't speak their language; I don't know the culture; and there's no one here to help me.' It was definitely a very bad idea to travel separately … or was this part of Kwame's plan? Tony knew that he must stay calm. It was a relief that in the room, there were also two other detainees – other flight passengers.

The room was even more gloomy than the airport lounge. It only had one window, which faced the lounge and two tubular fluorescent lights. There were two tables. At one table, sat a man in an airport uniform and a woman in a white medical outfit. The second table had two other men, both in civilian clothes. The two passengers were still standing at the table … a total of nine people in the room.

'May I ask what's going on?' Tony coughed as the muscles around his neck seemed to tighten. 'Why am I in here?' There was no answer, but he could hear the woman telling the two European passengers that they could leave the room.

'Ok!' said the woman at the desk, who finally acknowledged him. 'Give me your yellow medical book. In it there should be your immunisation records for cholera and yellow fever.' The immigration officer, who was still holding Tony's passport and the pamphlet stepped forward and handed them to her. She looked at the pamphlet with a frown and said, 'What is this?! This is not a medical book!' She paused as she looked towards her other colleague seated beside her. Looking back at Tony, she asked, 'Who said you could use this here?'

'That's what the embassy gave me!' replied Tony, nervously.

She opened the folder in front of her and retorted, 'Well, unfortunately, this has no value and you need to get your immunisation card before you can enter the country!'

'What?' exclaimed Tony. 'How I am supposed to get that now I'm already here?' The woman and her colleague burst out laughing. Astonished at their amusement, Tony started to contemplate what to do. He couldn't call Kwame, because he was already on a flight; he also had no idea whether his Weatherpool number would work from here. Tony realised how ill-prepared he was for this trip and business venture. He put his head in his hands and said under his breath, 'I knew I should have got Nicky involved'. He was aware that, together, they would have been able to avoid this situation.

'Don't worry!' said the man sitting next to her. 'That's why we are here!' His sonorous voice silenced the room. 'We can give you the yellow medical book with the immunisations that you need to enter the country!' He paused ... 'However, it will cost you one hundred and fifty dollars!'

'How much?' His voice cracked under the stress of the situation. 'Seriously, one hundred and fifty dollars!?'

'Yes! Just remember, you cannot enter the country without this document!' the man enforced.

Tony's thoughts were racing ... what was he supposed to do? He had no one to ask for any advice. He remembered that he had a substantial amount of cash on him. He put his hand into his pocket. He peeled eight notes off the roll of cash using his index finger. He pulled the notes out of his pocket and handed them over to the man, who unfolded and counted them.

'Ok, there's one hundred and sixty!' He looked towards the lady in the medical outfit. She then proceeded to open a file cabinet drawer underneath the table. From the drawer she took out a small yellow book with the words 'International Medical Book' on the cover. She then looked at Tony's passport and wrote his name and the date on the first page. She then ticked the two boxes in the immunisation columns labelled cholera and yellow fever.

She looked at Tony and exclaimed, 'This isn't a bank and we don't have any money to give back to you so we will keep the change'.

Tony looked at the woman in disbelief. There was another chorus of laughter from the airport staff in the room. The woman handed Tony the yellow book, his passport, and the pamphlet and said ' Ok! You may go!'

'What?!' said Tony, exasperated. 'Is that it? I don't get any injections or immunisations?' Their eyes widened as they pretended not to understand. The sniggers and laughter continued. Tony realised that he'd been conned. He turned away from the group at the desk, pulled the door open angrily, and walked out into the lounge. He couldn't believe that Kwame had set him up like that. They could've asked for more money, so he was probably lucky in that respect. As he walked through the door and out of the room, the immigration officer called after him, 'By the way … you need to get back in the queue.'

Tony stood in the queue, now at the back of

course, and continued to wait his turn to register with the immigration office and leave the airport. It seemed to him that everyone and everything had a price. Unlike Europe, here, you could buy anything you wanted if you knew the right people. When Tony finally reached the immigration counter an hour later, he presented the officer with his passport, his visa, and the yellow International Medical Book with its fake immunisation record.

The immigration officer looked through the documents and asked Tony 'What is your reason for visiting the country?' Unsure whether this was another con to get more cash out of him, Tony replied, 'I'm just here to see the beautiful scenery and do what tourists do best!' The officer looked at Tony, and with a steely look, he returned the document and said, 'You can go.'

Tony gripped his passport and yellow book and walked briskly away from the counter, following the other passengers towards the exit that would take him out of the airport. He needed to get to the restaurant at which he was supposed to be meeting Kwame.

He exited the building, and, with relief turned his phone on, from its airplane mode. He noticed there was no network showing on his phone. 'Great!' he said to himself. 'Now I'm in a foreign country, I don't understand the language, and I can't contact anyone here or in Weatherpool. Absolute madness!'

Tony decided that it would be better for him if he spoke to no one else. He made his way to the restaurant and went straight in. He walked up to the bar and perched on a high stool against the counter. A barman came over and asked, 'What for you, sir?'

Tony paused while he peered behind the man, looking at the beers on offer. 'I'll have a Singha, thank you!' The barman turned around and pulled one from the fridge. 'That's a ten, Sir!' he exclaimed. Tony pulled a twenty-dollar note from his left pocket using his left hand and leaned forward to hand over the money. Tony was taken aback when the barman moved away, still holding his beer.

Confused, Tony asked 'What's wrong? I'm sorry this is the smallest note I have!'

A gentleman sitting next to Tony at the bar turned to look at him, and said. 'You must be new to here! You can't use your left hand to pay! Your money will only be accepted if you pass it over with your right hand.'

'Oh ... right ... yeah. Thanks, it's my first time in Sanibo.' As he switched the money from his left hand to his right, the barman returned the beer to the counter and accepted the note, also returning Tony's change with his right hand. 'Very peculiar! Tony mused, nodding at the barman.

'I guess there's a lot to learn about the culture here!' Tony's mind drifted to everything that had happened since he'd arrived in West Africa. He looked down at his phone to see if the network was available, but it wasn't. He stared at the wall for a few seconds and then looked around the room, noticing the many different ethnicities in the restaurant. It was clear that people from all over the world came to the area either to do business or live here. Fifteen minutes must have passed as his beer was nearly finished, and still Kwame was nowhere to be seen. 'Have I been scammed?!' Tony thought to himself. 'I should probably figure out how to get back to the Weatherpool. I'm not staying here for seven days if he's not coming.'

Tony slid off his seat at the bar, grabbed his holdall, and started to walk towards the door, looking again at his phone to check for network service. 'Where am I going to go?' he thought to himself. Just as he reached out to pull the handle on the door, it opened and in burst Kwame, almost knocking him off his feet.

'Teach!' exclaimed the smiling man as he saw Tony in front of him. Tony replied, 'Thank goodness you're here!' I thought something had happened and you weren't coming!'

'I'm sorry I kept you waiting! Come and sit down,' said Kwame, jerking his head in the direction of the bar. Kwame sat on one of the bar stools and lifted his holdall on top of the large suitcase he had dragged in with him.

Shocked at the amount of luggage that Kwame had brought with him, Tony exclaimed, 'That's a lot of stuff!'

'Nah, not really', he replied, patting the suitcase and giving Tony a sly wink. 'I brought some stuff for the folks in Sanibo, the village we are going to, especially the Chief. This is how we will get what we came for without spending a lot of money'.

Tony looked curiously at the bags, but it was clear that Kwame wasn't going to tell him anything else just yet.

Kwame asked the barman for two beers, and held out a twenty-dollar note to pay for it. 'By the way, did you know that you have to pass money with....'

'Yeah, yeah!' Tony interrupted, 'with your right hand. I learned that the hard way.'

Kwame chuckled at Tony and handed the barman the money. They both picked up their drinks and continued to talk.

'How was your flight, Teach?' he asked.

'It was ok ...' He decided not to tell him anything about the yellow book at this point. Perhaps he would have that conversation another time. They chatted for a while about their journeys, then as Tony put his empty glass down on the bar, he looked out at the huge car park and its diverse selection of taxis and private vehicles that were busy collecting customers, friends, and relatives.

'So where do we go from here?' Tony asked.

'We'll take a taxi to the nearest village, Kinboasi and stay at a local hotel!' Kwame replied. 'Come on', he said. 'Let's go and find someone to take us now'.

They walked outside, and immediately, Kwame waved down a hideous red, brown, and green car with a 'Taxi' sign on the side. As it came closer, Tony realised that the car was hardly roadworthy. 'You've got to be kidding me …' he thought.

'We'll take this one!' Kwame muttered, seemingly ignoring the fact that it was dented all over and covered in rust and holes.

'Come on,' he said to Tony, who was understandably hesitant. 'Let's get in'.

Kwame attempted to open the damaged door at the back of the car. As it opened, the door was apparently only fixed by one hinge at the top. The taxi driver got out and picked up the suitcase and holdall belonging to Kwame, who was happy for him to place it in the boot. He reached out for Tony's, but he quickly refused, saying that he would keep hold of it. Tony thought to himself, 'Am I seriously the only one who is worried about the state of this car??'

'Teach!' said Kwame, interrupting Tony's thoughts. 'Get in! Let's go!'

Tony opened the rusty metal door and got in, tentatively sitting on a wobbly seat covered with layers of old bath towels and bed linen. This was going to be one unique taxi ride!

They set off very uncomfortably and the ramshackle taxi bumped and rattled its way along the dusty, uneven road. When they joined the main road, they moved slowly alongside the more modern cars, whilst the driver and Kwame locked horns in an intense discussion in their native African language. They navigated through the busy traffic then exited onto a road lined with rows of orange trees. The countryside came alive with the smell of the colourful fruits. Tony noticed a row of stalls full of ornate craftwork and behind them stood local people, selling their work, probably for a very low price.

The rusty car trudged to an eventual stop. Tony wondered why they had pulled up here. 'It's in the middle of nowhere', he thought to himself. Kwame shouted to Tony from the front of the car.

'He just wants to check his engine ... he says it's losing power. I don't think he realised how far we would be driving today.' Tony raised his eyebrows. He wasn't surprised. Kwame paused, then continued 'You see, he is a local driver and we've given him a profitable job ... by normal standards, it would take him five days to earn this amount of money. I think we'll keep him on as our personal driver.'

'Whatever you say,' said Tony despondently. The taxi driver walked to the rear of the car and towards the roadside bushes. Tony watched him squeeze through a slight opening between rows of tawny coloured banana trees, before disappearing from sight.

'Umm ... Kwame ... our driver has just disappeared,' said Tony in disbelief.

Turning around and peering through the

passenger window, Kwame replied 'Oh ... well, he said that his mechanic friend lives around here.'

The two men looked around, but couldn't possibly see where the driver's friend could live. There were no signs of life other than the neatly planted rows of tropical trees.

Kwame croaked, 'We haven't paid him yet! Surely he hasn't abandoned us!'

'Let's hope not! Tony replied, squinting through the dirt on the rear window.

A few minutes later the driver and another man emerged from the bushes in front of the car. Tony was amazed that someone was living in that remote area. He still couldn't see any other houses or any kind of community. The man approached the front of the aged vehicle and proceeded to lift the bonnet, which protested noisily as the rusty metal hinges were forced open.

Kwame alighted from the vehicle and catapulted some African words at the driver. Even though Tony didn't understand what he was saying, it was clear that he was annoyed with the driver for disappearing without telling us where he was going. The driver seemed to apologise as he pointed to his friend beside him. The man laughed and continued his examination of the indisposed vehicle.

To Tony's amazement, the man performed mechanical surgery on the ailing vehicle using two wires, a lightbulb, and a screwdriver. Tony thought to himself, 'This man is using his ordinary human knowledge to do something extraordinary. In Weatherpool, a mechanic would require computer diagnostics!' After thirty minutes of jostling with engine, moving backward and forward from one side to another, and with short bursts of activity in the driver's cockpit, the man took a step back as the exhaust pipe belched out a billow of black smoke.

'That should do it!' chuckled the mechanic, who looked very pleased with himself. A three-way conversation continued, ending with Kwame handing our driver a stack of bank notes. From which, the driver proffered some to the mechanic, who took them gratefully. Tony could only look on as he had no idea about what was being said. He was pretty sure it was nothing to do with diamonds. The taxi driver dropped the bonnet with a crash and the three men got back in the taxi. Tony wondered whether it would get them to their destination, but as the driver put his foot on the accelerator, the car lurched forward with gusto, throwing Tony backwards and off his pile of towels. Kwame turned round and saw Tony trying to get back into an upright position and laughed.

'You OK back there, Teach?' he joked. Tony looked at him and grunted a response as he hauled himself back up on to the seat. 'Hmmm...' he murmured.

They continued for another twenty minutes or so, before arriving at an intersection that led to three incongruous clay-covered roads. On either side of knee-high shrubs, there were old tyre tracks, a clear sign that the path was rarely used, and even then, by a small amount of traffic. The rust bucket stopped for few seconds as the driver contemplated the crossroads; he swung the car round onto the roadway on the left, before muttering something in African to Kwame.

Looking at his watch, Kwame responded 'Um, ok!'

He turned round to look at Tony and said, 'Teach, we'll be at Kinboasi in ten minutes!' He then went on to explain the plan of action. First, they would meet the Chief of the village; he was an old friend of Kwame's and the intended recipient of the suitcase's contents. Kwame told Tony that, in the suitcase, there were clothes, shoes, handbags, perfume, and other accessories for him and for the ladies in the village. He explained that they would also give the Chief a sum of money. This would guarantee obtaining the precious stones at a price lower than their market value and would give them an important status whilst they were staying in the village.

The taxi rattled at pace around the curve, its wing mirror brushing against the metre-high grass. The car's underbelly mowed the top of the trampled weeds that grew down the centre of the clay road. They travelled like this for a few minutes before entering a clearing, from which they could see scattered houses in the distance and a scattering of wildlife in nearby fields. The driver slowed right down whilst looking for the residence of Kwame's friend, the village Chief. About halfway through the village, the driver turned into a nicely manicured lawned yard with a large lemon-coloured house to the rear and two pale blue houses up at the front; the two nearest houses were in disrepair, one requiring more work than the other. The large yellow house at the back, which was constructed from timber, bricks, and concrete was the most opulent house they had seen so far in the village.

The car rattled to a stop between the two blue houses; as the men were about to get out of the car, three mean-looking dogs bolted over, snarling and barking.

'I'm staying in the rust bucket!' said Tony out loud. He would rather be uncomfortable than ripped to shreds.

The front door of the yellow house opened, and a large man wearing a traditional African dress alighted; from the other two houses, came two other men in colourful attire. One of the men who came out of the blue houses, patted his leg with his palm and whistled. The dogs immediately ran towards him. That was their cue to get out of the car; Kwame was the first to open his partly unhinged door. He stepped out onto the carpet of grass.

'Bajjo!' said Kwame, who then continued to speak in his native tongue to the man from the yellow house.

'Is that you Kwame?' the man replied in English. 'You have grown!' A few more words were exchanged in the African tongue, and everyone started to laugh, except Tony of course. He didn't understand what they were saying, but he decided to join in with the laughter as he didn't want to look out of place. Kwame walked towards the large man who had now descended the flight of stairs and was standing on the bottom step.

Kwame paused and turned to Tony. 'Teach, can you get the suitcase from the boot?'

'Sure!' Tony replied as he tapped the driver on the shoulder. 'Help me get this open will you?' He nodded and they stepped back and approached the car. The driver obviously had a knack for opening the boot. He gave it a shove and hit it in a particular spot with his fist. As the boot lifted, he smiled at Tony and hauled out the huge suitcase.

'I can take it from here!' Tony exclaimed, as he grabbed the handle of the suitcase, pulling it along to where Kwame was stood waiting for him to catch-up. As he dragged it along and passed it over to Kwame, Tony panted, 'It's really heavy!'

With a few more steps, they were both standing just below the step on which the chief stood.

'Bajjo, this is Tony!' said Kwame pointing towards the teacher, 'He's a friend of mine!' The Chief looked at Tony, who was still panting from dragging the case across the yard, then over Kwame's shoulder, towards the taxi and its driver. He raised his eyebrows out of curiosity. Kwame responded, 'Ah, the other chap is our driver! But ... most importantly Bajjo... this suitcase is for you!'

The Chief Bajjo laughed, 'You haven't forgotten your manners then?!' You've remembered how to look after your Chief. Let's go inside!'

The Chief turned and headed towards the front door as we ascended the steps. We reached the top high stairs and stepped onto a long veranda with three seats positioned so they were overlooking the yard.

As they approached the door, it seemed to open automatically, but Tony realised on entering that a tall thin man had opened it as he saw them approaching. The same man took hold of the suitcase as Tony was about to pass it to him. Impatiently, the man snapped 'I'll take that.'

The man lifted the suitcase effortlessly with one hand as if it was empty. Looking at the case, Bajjo asked 'So what have you brought for me?!'

'Just the things that I know you and your people need,' said Kwame.

The conversation between Kwame and the Chief continued for about ten minutes. While they chatted, Kwame opened the suitcase and showed the Chief all of the goodies. There were men's and women's shoes and boots, jeans, branded t-shirts, ladies' underwear, and dresses. Kwame also gave the Chief a bundle of bank notes, which would pay for the diamonds and hospitable treatment they would receive. As they continued their conversation,

Tony looked around at the décor or the house and all the lavish items that were in it. Whilst some of the furniture looked ordinary, there was noticeable glittering gold incorporated into almost everything. As a centrepiece on the coffee table, stood a clump of untamed metal the size of a tennis ball. Around the room there were many similar natural and sculptured gold items.

The wealth of the Chief was evident but simplistic and Tony doubted that the Chief understood the value of his wealth in EU or US terms. Kwame explained to the Chief how many diamonds he required and asked how often they would need to travel to and from West African village to retrieve them.

The plan for this trip was to hide small diamonds, one hundred and twenty carats altogether, in laptop batteries. The batteries would be emptied out and filled with diamonds. The principle behind this idea was that two laptops would be shipped to Weatherpool via an international parcel company. The men were aware that they would be scanned multiple times. So to further disguise the diamonds hidden within the batteries, the batteries would be coated with carbon paper before reinserting them back into the plastic housing. The chemical makeup of diamonds is naturally hardened carbon. This strategy meant that the diamonds wouldn't be seen or detected when the laptops were is put through a scanner. It would appear that the batteries were made of the normal components. The only setback was that the laptops wouldn't have any power if customs checked whether they were working. However, on the paperwork it would state that they required repairs, hence the reason for sending them Weatherpool. Ingenious! On another note, exporting diamonds without a Kimberley Certificate is illegal in West Africa. A certificate would cost over one hundred thousand dollars and would be overseen by international authorities and procedures. Whilst the locals would not be able to afford to buy such a certificate or refine the diamonds themselves, the market price at the source was very low. In Europe, a certified rough ten carat diamond, depending on its clarity and colour, is worth hundreds of thousands of dollars, but here, in Kinboasi, because it is uncertified, and doesn't fall within the international definition of blood diamonds, it's priced at a few hundred dollars, around the same price that you would expected to pay for a branded pair of sports shoes in the US or Europe. Tony found it difficult to believe that these local people had access to all of these precious resources but were still poor.

The extended conversation between Kwame and chief had mellowed and there were several moments of spontaneous laugher. Eventually, Kwame addressed Tony as they got up from their seats.

'Come on, Teach. Bajjo is taking us to the local bar for drinks and entertainment after we've completed our business today. The sooner we get started, the sooner the local girls can teach you a thing or two about African hospitality, ha ha!'

The group exited the front door, which again was 'automatically' opened by the tall thin man. The Chief trundled ahead, checking his mobile phone and initiating a call to someone in his local dialect. It was clear that the chief's conversation was directly related to Kwame and Tony and their reason for being in Africa. The Chief ended the call, turned to two men and said, 'We will meet Mama Owusu, so make sure you will have some money to deal with whatever she shows you!'

Kwame's face lit up, 'Did you hear that, Teach?'

'Sure!' Tony replied. 'But what does he mean?'

Kwame snapped his fingers and said, 'Teach, we will have some stones in our hands tonight! This is why we are here and Bajjo doesn't mess around!'

The group of men descended the steps, following the chief through the clay paved yard, past the battered taxi that they arrived in, and onto a gravel-surfaced road that led to a more populated part of the village. Houses were littered on both sides of the road, but none were as flamboyant as those in Weatherpool; these were more like shacks. Bajjo and his entourage of three were treated as royalty as they walked along the road. People came forward and bowed their heads slightly out of respect. Their first stop was a house that was no bigger than thirty square metres; it was mainly made from treated timber and the floor was a mixture of wood and concrete. In some parts the yellow and blue paint peeled back to reveal rotting bare wood underneath.

A Bajjo stopped, his entourage halted behind him. He shouted 'Mama Owusu ... ! Mamaaa!' His long singing tone was interrupted by the opening of the creaky front door.

'Bajjo!' said an elderly woman standing in the doorway.

In response, Bajjo stated 'Mama, these are the men I told you about over the phone. Do you have the stones?' Then breaking off into an African tongue, the elderly lady turned around and went back into her house. Bajjo beckoned us to follow him. They climbed two short sets of steps and entered the small dwelling. The house was neatly decorated with wooden furniture, including ornate rocking chair, on which Mama Owusu was already seated. There was a sofa with two seats and another armchair to the right of the rocking chair. Kwame and Tony sat on the sofa, giving the Chief opportunity to occupy the armchair next to them.

There was a brief conversation between the Chief and Mama Owusu, before she placed her right hand down her loose top and into her cleavage from which she pull out a calico brown cloth the size of a tennis ball. She handed it to the Chief; his hands gripped the bag as he muttered something to her in African. He then passed the bag to Kwame, who sitting directly in front of him.

Kwame gently held the folded calico cloth in his left palm and started unfolding the wrap with his right hand. Tony looked on in amazement, curious to see what was going to be revealed.

'Wow!' exclaimed Kwame, as he saw handful of glinting stones. 'You see this Teach?' Kwame looked up at Mama Owusu and asked 'How much, Mama? How much?' The elderly lady looked at the Chief.

In response, the Chief said 'She won't sell all of them. You see these are her savings and she depends on these stones to feed herself and grandchildren. So, you can take any six from what you see there in return for eight thousand!'

Kwame looked at me, 'Teach I have no idea how many carats six will be...! Let's weigh six of the clearer stones!'

As Kwame placed the parcel of stones on the floor Tony could see that that there were about twenty or so similar stones on the cloth. They were all crystal clear and reflected what little light there was in the room. The elderly woman bent forward in her rocking chair and spoke in African to Kwame. He nodded his head and moved back a little to allow her to select six of the stones.

She muttered, 'Thirty seven, thirty eight...'

Kwame took the small scale that Tony had removed from his bag. As he placed seven stone on the scale the numbers totted up to thirty-eight point six-five carats. 'Mama you are right!' said KWAME as the elderly lady laughed in amusement.

Kwame turned to look at Tony. 'Ok, Teach, we need to pay her what Bajjo said!'

Tony reached into the bag he was carrying and opened a wash bag; some of their money was in here. The rest was concealed in different pockets and openings of Tony's clothing so it would be less likely detected when going through customs. Tony carefully removed the bank notes and handed them to Kwame in stacks of thousands. Kwame confirmed the amount by double counting the notes then handed them to the Chief for a third verification before finally handing the notes to Mama Owusu. Whilst the moneys were being checked and handed over, Kwame quickly took the seven stones, placing them into black jewellery bags and passing them to Tony, who tucked them into his front left pocket.

While Kwame, Bajjo and Mama chatted in African, Tony zoned out to do some rough calculations of his own. It was clear that they had just done a fantastic deal; the seven rough stones were worth more than one hundred thousand dollars and they had just paid eight thousand for them. He realised that this trip was going to be very profitable ... the only downside to the deal would be Thaddeus. He had demanded fifty percent of whatever they would gain from this venture, because he had introduced Tony to Kwame. He supposed it would still be worth it if his predicted calculations were correct. After about ten minutes, Bajjo got up from the armchair and proceeded towards the front door. 'Let's go! We have others to see and no time to waste! It's better to get this done today then tomorrow you can relax and enjoy some entertainment.' He winked at Tony when he said this, and threw his head back as he laughed heartily.

They walked past another two houses before stopping. Bajjo knocked on the front door of another small thatched house, from which an elderly man alighted, leaning on a walking stick. The process here was much the same as it was with Mama. However, this man's stones were hidden in an old copper pot underneath the floorboards. The elderly man had many more than Mama, but most were not as clear and too big, at least fifteen carats or more per stone, which would have never fitted into the laptop battery housing. So, from him, they could only accept two stones totalling ten point six carats. They continued through the village, visiting another six houses as well as entering into conversations with other individuals they met on the footpaths. The men found it an astonishing experience as they examined the crystallised stones that were being presented to them by young people and the elderly;

they were amazed at how these people seemed so unaware of the wealth they had.

It was a fruitful day, yielding nearly one hundred and eighty carats. Kwame and Tony had managed to buy a mixture of crystals from clear to slightly opaque and two large diamonds at just over six point eight carats. To finish the day, Bajjo took us to the only restaurant and bar in the village, which was actually an annex attached to the house of its owner. In the bar, there were several men playing dominoes or checkers; bizarrely, even though they were in a public house with a bar, no-one had a drink on their table. They were, however, in a joyous mood, seemingly enjoying the last of the daylight. As they approached the open air section of the bar where most of the men played, the men greeted the Chief reverently and cleared a path to the counter. Some even got up and cleared a table so that Bajjo could sit down with his entourage. The men also afforded a nod to the other members of the Chief's party.

The silence and the change in mood of the players must have alerted the bar's owner, because he suddenly appeared and stood beside the Chief before he had chance to sit at the table.

Looking round at the short, stocky man, Bajjo exclaimed 'Hey, John! 'These are my guests; they will need two rooms tonight and some entertainment!'

'Ok! No problem at all!' said the chubby faced owner, nodded respectfully at the Chief.

To Kwame and Tony, the Chief authoritatively explained, 'You will both stay here tonight and John will look after you; that way, you can drink as much as you want without worrying about how you're going to get back to my place. I will pick you up in the morning and we can continue from where we left off.'

He continue, 'Don't worry about safety, either. Now that you're in this village as my guests, nothing will happen to you. Actually, I'll rephrase that … only GOOD things will happen to you whilst you are my guests!'

The chief turned to John and spoke in African. John walked over to the bar, opened the fridge and removed a few bottles of beer. He then took two bottles, whiskey and brandy, from the higher shelves.

This place was a world away from Weatherpool and Tony was enjoying the new and unusual experience. The thing that struck him the most was how happy and calm the people were, even though they didn't have the modern facilities that we take for granted. They were satisfied and content with what they had. They had untold wealth in the diamonds they owned in their village; they owned enough to build a modern city with its luxurious trappings. But their simplicity and acceptance of the fact that they shouldn't sacrifice wealth at the expense of destroying their environment was admirable. Their interest in the sale of diamonds was only a direct result of people like Tony and Kwame, who had invaded their culture with offers of money for the precious stones.

Time had moved forward so quickly and, suddenly, their thoughts were disrupted with the softer tones of women, who had been called for by the Chief through John. Looking around the room, Tony realised there were now more women than men. The women were of various ages and sizes.

The youngest had only recently crossed over into the threshold of puberty. This was, in itself, a cultural difference that required an open mind-set; here, the age of consent was left to the individual's readiness to enter into a mature conversation and sexual relationship, based on her own likes, dislikes, agendas, circumstances and mental and physical development. This was all provided at a reasonable financial cost for the men's enjoyment. Tony decided that it wasn't for him. He downed a couple of drinks then made his excuses and wandered off to the dimly lit bedroom he had been given for the next few days, while Kwame and the Chief took advantage of the ladies.

Tony rose with the daylight and checked his phone hoping for a network connection, but there was none. This reflected how isolated they were. Tony sat and thought about Nicky and what he might be doing in his organisation for the Brink's Heist. Both jobs were a twinned effort and, if both plans came to fruition, the success and wealth would be theirs.

Days had now passed and Tony had started to adjust to the village lifestyle of Kinboasi. He and Kwame could now find their way around without being escorted by the Chief. Being aware of who they were, the locals showed them the same level of respect as they did for the important man they had arrived with. Tony made two new friends: Keto and Pabo. Both were sons of the Chief by different mothers and were two of his thirteen children. Keto was also a protector in the village; even though the village was peaceful, there were undercurrents of secrets and rivalries with the neighbouring village. It wasn't too obvious, but it turned out that most of the men in the village carried concealed firearms and were ex-military. Some had been involved in past civil wars, largely to protect their loved ones. The stories of heroism were marked on the skin in the form of battle scars from head wounds to disfigured hands with missing fingers. Keto and Pabo were both parents themselves with limited earnings. Without telling Kwame, Tony intended making a meaningful financial contribution to both of these men to alleviate some of the pressures that their young families were facing. He also promised them that, on his return, he would bring a suitcase of shoes, clothes and accessories for them and their respective families.

Through the Chief, Tony and Kwame organised someone from the shipping company to come to the village to collect and freight the laptops to Weatherpool. The gentleman who agreed to do this also returned to the village and gave them a copy of the shipping invoice. That confirmed that the laptops were sent to Weatherpool and would arrive within five working days, two days after we returned. It was time to head back to Weatherpool; Tony felt quite sad as it had been an experience of a lifetime; he had wallowed in the unique lifestyle and environment in the village. Saying that, as he hadn't understood much of what was said during his time there, he couldn't have known if anything sinister was happening. He was aware that there was something bubbling underneath the surface in the African village. He wondered whether this would be revealed during future trips to Sanibo and Kinboasi, West Africa.

CHAPTER SIX

Tony's flight arrived at Fleming airport, which was one hour and five minutes away from Weatherpool by car. It was a really pleasant feeling to be back in a familiar place, without the need for translation or navigation around poisonous vines. There were enough beastly characters and horrors to deal with in Weatherpool, without the strange sights and smells and awkward low-toned conversations he had just experienced in Africa.

The two men usually picked each other up at the airport if either of them travelled abroad, so Tony was expecting to see Nicky waiting in the arrival lounge, ready to receive an update on the diamond job. Tony knew that Nicky would be impressed by the successful visit to Kinboasi. Likewise, he hoped he would be equally enraptured by the progress Nicky had made regarding the heist.

Tony whizzed through the terminal scanner and briefly acknowledged the immigration officials. There were many benefits of traveling light; you can almost glide through to the arrival lounge avoiding the hassle in the baggage hall and the annoying questions from custom officers, who ask, repeatedly, 'Anything to declare?'

Entering the lounge, Tony was two kilograms lighter than when he left to travel to West Africa, but his muscle mass was still intact. He was ready for a good meal. He looked around the brightly light lounge hoping to see Nicky waiting on one of the maroon sofas. But he wasn't in sight … that said, it had been nearly ten days since he'd last heard from him.

'I hope nothing bad has happened!' thought Tony to himself. He checked his phone for any messages or missed calls. This was not what he expected at all. Tony walked around checking the lounge bars and cafes to see if Nicky had somehow miss-timed his arrival and had decided to have something to eat … but he was still nowhere to be seen.

'This is odd!' Tony thought.

'I'll try WhatsApp. That's probably the best way to find out where he is', he muttered to himself. He quickly typed 'I'm at the airport!' and waited for the message status to show that it had been delivered. Tony waited for another minute, before sending another message that read simply, 'Are you ok?'

Both messages had been delivered, but the app wasn't showing when Nicky was last online. Tony decided to wait for fifteen more minutes before deciding to take a taxi home. He soon became weary from walking around the lounge, and found himself sitting on a maroon sofa staring at the exit doors. His stare was interrupted by a message alert on his phone. It was a message from Nicky. It just said, '10'.

Tony, taken aback, thought, 'Wow, OK.' He realised that Nicky must be caught up with something important, so he replied with just two letters, 'C U'.

Something wasn't right at all and his gut began to sink. Tony's imagination drifted off into all sorts of dramatic possibilities. 'It must be something important if he's not made it to the airport to meet me,' he thought.

Tony had waited for almost an hour, when his phone rang. It was Nicky. Relieved, Tony picked up the phone, clicked the green button and exclaimed, 'Hey! Wha..', but was immediately interrupted by Nicky's panicking voice.

'I'm at the airport at the pickup point ... I'm in the Merc ... we have a meeting with Thaddeus and his crew at the barn, so we need to hurry. I wanna get there before they do so we have a chance to talk.' Nicky ended the call without giving Tony a chance to respond.

Tony hastily grabbed his bag and ran to the exit. The Mercedes was there, parked clumsily in the pickup bay with its engine running and the front passenger door open. Tony ran and hopped into the front, tossing his bag at his feet; the vehicle was in motion before he could close the door.

'Teach, there is so much shit going on!! We have most of the money stacked and ready to deal with the Brinks job, but everyone is getting greedy! In the end, we'll be lucky to get a penny out of this!'

Nicky rambled on saying that Thaddeus had taken over everything and that their meeting today was supposed to give them more information about what will happen next and how things will be done.

He paused as he overtook a line of six vehicles. He hit the top of steering wheel with his lower palm in frustration. He continued, 'I gave Mikey, one of Thaddeus' soldiers, the angel dust and, apparently, we'll get the money for that today!'

Tony didn't have much of a chance to update Nicky about the trip to West Africa; Nicky continued to gabble on about all of the challenges he had faced on his own while he was away. Tony got the impression that what had started off as a good business plan, had now turned out to be the worst business decision they had made so far.

Nicky must have been distracted by all the unpleasant events he was explaining, as when they approached the path that led to the old barn, he seemed to suddenly jolt into consciousness. He slammed on the brakes and made a U-turn onto the narrow path. It was the first time Tony had ever seen Nicky so unsettled. It bothered him, because it was clear that Nicky wasn't telling him everything.

Their vehicle slowed down to a crawl on the path to the old barn. It's tyres crunched the dry hay that lay on the familiar parking area in front of the dilapidated building. The Merc took the total number of vehicles parked at the barn up to five. The two men got out of the car and as they moved towards the rear of the vehicle they could hear a heated conversation behind the bushes.

'This way, Teach!' said Nicky, quietly. 'Thaddeus said that they'd be at the back, underneath the willow tree!' They made their way round to the back of the building, stepping over the rusty truck axles and rims that had been embedded into the ground.

'Just over there, I can see them!' Nicky pointed; he paused to check his phone. Tony's attention was focused on the people under the willow tree. They sat at arm's length from each other on bales of hay used to create makeshift seats. At a glance, there were four men and three women. The men sitting opposite each other were separated by a thin sack covering another dried hay bale. On it were empty beer bottles and a quantity of dark coloured spirits.

The closer they got to the willow tree, the louder the voices of Thaddeus and his crew became. They looked at each other and then at Nicky and Tony. Thaddeus stood up and walked quickly towards Nicky, stopping only five centimetres away from his face. He stared at him up close and shouted, 'Next time you have business to do, DON'T use MY soldiers!'

He paused, then continued, 'You come to ME,

first! GET IT?!' Thaddeus looked back at Mikey, who was supposed to pay Nicky for the angel dust. In a split second, Thaddeus had pushed Nicky backwards, picked up a sheet of hay off the ground, and swung round whilst pulling a three fifty-seven magnum from his waist. Thaddeus was now standing behind Mikey pushing the sheet of hay against his back. The gun in his left hand anchored the hay; looking round and glaring at Nicky, Thaddeus pumped three muffled shots into Mikey's back. He then pushed Mikey's body forward and it slumped onto the makeshift table, knocking the bottles onto the ground.

'Fucking hell!!' Tony shouted, and, in shock, he stepped backwards. Nicky eyes widened in horror at what they had just witnessed. 'You're fucking mad!' he shouted through gritted teeth. The three women huddled together on the hay bales and the other two men stoop up, unfazed. Thaddeus handed the gun over to one of the men, who removed a cloth from his back pocket and started to clean the gun to remove Thaddeus's fingerprints. Nicky and Tony looked on in shock.

The Lucifer figure laughed, looking at Nicky.

'You see what YOU did?' He laughed again, 'YOU just killed Mikey in front of six witnesses, and Chandler here, HE'S a police officer!!' he shouted, pointing at a burly man standing with his hands by his side, ready to pull his weapon if needed.

Nicky and Tony glanced at each other. They realised that this was the beginning of the end. Whatever happened from now on would be unimaginable. They watched as Thaddeus's men wrapped up the body in a tarpaulin. One of the men placed the three fifty-seven magnum in a clear plastic evidence bag.

Thaddeus walked towards them and grunted, 'Remember now ... the two of you are working for me ... you will give me all the diamonds! Make sure that whenever I call, you pick up and answer. Oh, and thanks for the angel dust! Now fuck off and wait for my call.'

Thaddeus spat on Tony's shoes then turned and headed back to supervise what the others were doing with the body. Without hesitation, the two friends turned around and made a hasty departure from the grotesque scene underneath the willow tree. They had have never been so shaken by anything. For the first time, they felt defeated and lost in a fog of bewilderment and irony from the unexpected event.

They got back into their vehicle confused at how things had got so out of their control; they had thought they were on track to make millions from smuggling diamonds and from the Brinks heist. It was like they'd been beaten at a game that they knew they were the experts at. Over the years, Nicky and Tony had been through a large number of challenging situations, thus, they had never underestimated their fortitude or resilience. They now needed time to collect their thoughts, but as they got into the Merc, they both knew without speaking that the only way to take control would be to kill Thaddeus and anyone else that got in their way.

'Bro, we should go to your place. We really need to think carefully about our next move', said Tony looking across at Nicky's ashen face.

'Yeah,' Nicky replied, staring at the empty road in front of them. 'Yeah, let's do that.'

Tony looked again at Nicky and saw his face muscles were taut. The silence in the car was deafening. The two men stared ahead as if it wasn't just the road they were looking for, but their futures. They remained in this silent trance for the full forty-eight minutes that it took to arrive at Nicky's home in Free Port. They got out of the car, still not saying a word; they knew that they'd have to tell Marianna what had happened and, no doubt, she would form her own opinion on what should be done to fix the situation.

With everything that had happened, Tony hadn't had chance to tell Nicky about the West African village. It was certainly going to be a very long night. Nicky's yard was still littered with a mixture of crashed and stunningly repaired high-end vehicles. It was two hours until midnight, so Marianna should still be awake, either watching a series or preparing her lunch for tomorrow – one of her little routines.

The two men walked into the house, and Tony closed the door behind him with a click.

Still out of sight, Marianna called out, 'Hey

babe!' As they turned the corner of the hallway and came into view, she smiled at Nicky, said 'Oh, hi Tony', then looked back at the television captivated by her movie.

'Hey, sweetness!' replied Nicky, walking up behind the sofa and kissing Marianna on the cheek. Tony set his backpack down on the kitchen floor next to the dining table at which they had all sat on many previous occasions. Walking back into the kitchen, Nicky opened the refrigerator door and looked around at Tony. 'What would you like, Teach? Cider or lager?'

'I don't mind, as long as its strong and cold', he replied.

Marianna was still focused on her movie. Tony knew what was going on in Nicky's head; he would want to retaliate straight away for what Thaddeus had just done, but high emotions and knee-jerk reactions were not a good mix. The key to the friends' success so far was that they always thought carefully about long-term consequences, and, where possible, planned to avert them. That's why they had been so successful in the past and hadn't yet been caught out. This time should be no different and Tony was determined to keep them both focused.

'Tony sat down at the table. 'Nicky, so much has happened since I arrived at the airport and I'm guessing there's more to tell me … ?!' Nicky replied with a nod. Tony continued, ' … but I need to tell you what happened on my trip, especially now that we've got to hand all the diamonds over to Lucifer … I mean … Thaddeus', he said, shaking his head.

Tony went on to tell Nicky about the people in Kinboasi and the systems. He talked about the timeframe of the diamonds' arrival and how they would sell them. He realised now that all of this would be determined by Thaddeus and this frustrated him. He told his friend that the laptops were expected to arrive in two days, at which time they would have to hand everything over to their enemy.

Tony continued, 'We won't even be able to salvage a few for ourselves because Kwame would have told the boss how many carats we shipped. If the stones don't arrive safely, they will think we've stolen them because they're being posted to my home address. We can only hope that nothing bad happens and that they're delivered on time'.

The two men exchanged ideas and thoughts about the unfolding situation. They decided that they couldn't go through with the Brinks heist. They also knew that they must make as much as they could from the diamonds. The one thing they were clearest on, however, was that Thaddeus must be eliminated and there was only one way to do that.

Marianna had finished watching her film and had gone to bed a couple of hours before. Tony was on his sixth cider and Nicky had downed a similar number of lagers. The friends had, by this time, sketched out their plan and were ready to take action at daybreak.

The next morning, sunlight beamed through the kitchen window and a lingering smell of toast and coffee greeted Tony's senses as he opened his eyes. There was an eerie stillness inside Nicky's house as if an angel of death was present, a quietness that made him feel as if Thaddeus was inside his house. Tony and Nicky hadn't had any physical contact with Thaddeus the night before, but amongst the smell of morning toast and beverages, there was a faint odour of embalming fluid.

Tony jumped up from the sofa. He could see two mugs on the dining table and the kitchen curtains were partially open. The shadow from the strong sunlight indicated it was nearing midday. As he stood up from the sofa, the front door handle turned slowly, and the door was pushed open. His heart raced for a second, but he relaxed instantly when he saw it was Nicky.

'Morning, Teach', he said, seeing Tony standing up. 'I took Marianna to work and gave her the gist of what's going on … I didn't want to wake you. She agrees that we need to get out of this deal.'

He continued, 'She's offered to help us in any way she can.' With the door closed, he added the chain and bolted a secondary lock on the door. 'I gave her five thousand dollars' worth of counterfeit notes; she will post them to her bank's fraud office unanimously with details of Mr Chin's workshop on Molynes Road. Her bank's fraud department will contact the police headquarters, so there won't be any risk of them finding out who sent them. Thaddeus and his crew won't know the information came from us. Once Mr Chin's operation is closed down, the Brink's heist will be crippled.'

'Perfect!' replied Tony. 'Our next step will be to stop the diamond smuggling operation, but that won't be so easy. As we said last night, we will have to go with Kwame to Kinboasi. As soon as we receive the laptops, we will be able to see how the process works fully.'

Tony continued, 'We still have money left over from the Saunders's job we did, so we can invest extra and divert some of the diamonds. What do you think? Will Marianna come with us too?'

'No!' Nicky replied, forcefully. 'Definitely not. I wouldn't ask her to do such a thing!' He paused, then continued, 'Let's see how it turns out with the first set that comes in!'

They went into the open-plan kitchen. Nicky sat at the table and Tony opened the fridge to find something to drink. The smell of embalming fluid was much stronger near the fridge. He started to tell Nicky … 'You know what?' Stuttering, he stopped himself and said, 'Never mind!' He decided to say nothing about it.

'What is it, Teach?' Nicky looked up.

'Nothing ... I was just ... umm ... thinking about Thaddeus. He lives about one hundred metres up the river from my house, so it would be good idea to use the river as a route to execute our plans; if we walked or drove up there we would be seen for sure.'

'That's a brilliant idea!' Nicky replied. 'The waterway is perfect and it gets shallower the closer we get to his house!! We'll just have to do a tactical run and check out his place! When do you want to stake him out?'

The distinct smell of embalming fluid was still distracting and lingering. Tony couldn't believe that Nicky hadn't noticed it. He coughed and then replied, 'How about tonight? I think, the sooner the better!'

Nicky hesitated and took a deep breath before gasping, 'Yeah, why not.'

Tony felt that there was something that Nicky wasn't telling him. Tony took a lager from the fridge and gulped down a mouthful. They talked through the plans again, but Nicky still seemed distracted.

The two men each helped themselves to another drink from the fridge and decided to go out into the yard to have a look at two motorbikes that Nicky's Uncle Darren had recently modified. Since his accident, Tony had become very cautious and was much less of a risk taker ... but it was time that he got back on a motorbike. The two bikes in front of him were just begging to be tested. They were both orange and black with oversized tyres and modified chrome stainless steel tailpipes; this meant they'd be heard approaching from a mile away. Darren had also upgraded the fuel tanks, which gave them a macho look and feel. This also meant that they would be able to withstand faster speeds and cover much longer distances than standard motorbikes of that size. To complete the look, both vehicles came with orange and black half cut helmets with plaited chin straps, which allowed riders to talk to each other without removing their helmets.

They looked the bikes over and then sat on their soft black leather seats. 'These are just begging for a test run!' said Tony, fully aware that Nicky wouldn't approve because of the accident. Nicky was silent for a moment, but then he rubbed his hand over the tank and replied, 'Well, if you're up for it, Teach, I don't see why not. We all have to get over our fears at some point – the sooner the better, I guess!'

Nicky continued, 'I'll grab the keys and you come in and get your stuff! We'll head to your place and then get a move on with our plans!'

For ten minutes or so, they were like those young school children again playing in the fern field with Grace, excited about their adventures. Tony slung the long straps of the holdall over his shoulder allowing the weight of the bag to rest on the pillion seat. He put on his helmet and strapped it on securely, watching his friend do the same. It was time to set off on a road that would define their bond and fortitude.

The two friends started the bikes and set off. The power from the bikes took them by surprise and the oversized tyres skidded and propelled the gravel sideways and then out of the back. Tony could feel the horsepower between his legs and he tightened his quadriceps in response. Nicky was now one hundred metres ahead, weaving between the potholes that were peppered on the road from Free Port to the intersection that would take them through the town and onto the road to Weatherpool. Tony's rev counter reached four, as the gap between the two friends narrowed. He could now see Nicky's eyes in his rear view mirror. The noise from the tailpipes was so loud that it drowned the sounds of everything else around them.

Nicky lifted himself up so he was standing up on the bike, forced an extra rev, and lifted his front wheel off the ground into a wheelie. He really wanted to show off the power of the bike. Tony would not be taking that risk at this point. It was his first ride since the accident and his holdall would affect the weight distribution. He decided he would leave showing off until next time. After fifteen minutes of playing catch the leader, they slowed down to a mere crawl as they arrived at Fletchers Avenue, where Tony lived. Even though he had only been away for eleven days, he noticed changes to the neighbours lawns, a different car on a driveway, and gardens that needed grooming, including his own. On the roadside, three metres from Tony's gate, was parked a dark blue car with tinted windows. This was very unusual because no one in Weatherpool left their cars out on the street. Very odd. He pulled his bike up alongside Nicky's and said, 'I wonder who's that belongs to.'

'No idea! Nicky replied, equally puzzled.

Tony took the lead and drove past the vehicle, while trying to peer into the windscreen. Nicky, picking up the rear, did the same thing and realised it was the police officer that was at the old barn with Thaddeus. They continued towards Tony's driveway and pulled up so that Tony could open the automatic gate. Nicky said, 'I know who that was!' 'Me too', replied Tony. 'Chandler ... I would recognise him anywhere.'

Nicky quietly hissed under his breath, 'This is why we need to execute our plans. It looks like we're going to have to take care of the police now, too!'

Things were out of their control now. Tony could see the steadfast expression on Nicky's face and knew he was ready to explode. Knowing the type of person Thaddeus was, he wouldn't trust anyone else to dispose of Mikey's body. He would also keep hold of the gun. It was clear that he was sending them a message, on that said, 'DON'T mess with me.'

Tony pressed the automatic gate release button and the two men rode their bikes onto the driveway. The car pulled in behind them, uninvited. Tony shot off his bike, kicking the bike stand onto the concrete and stormed over to the driver's door. Nicky was equally furious and closely followed.

'What the fuck are you doing on my driveway!!? Tony spat saliva out of his mouth onto the closed window of the car. 'You're trespassing on private property. You'd better leave, RIGHT NOW!' he shouted angrily. Running past him, Nicky went round to the front passenger door just as the police officer quickly got out. He leaned on the door, resting his right hand on his firearm.

'What do you fucking pieces of shit think you're doing?! I'm just trying to deliver a message from the boss; we know you live here; if you try to make any stupid moves, you're both fucked; I'm telling you now, so back off! he retorted, aggressively. He continued, 'Just you make sure you hand over the diamonds when they arrive; if you don't, you know what's coming; not just for you, but also for your families!'

His message was clear; Nicky and Tony would have to act swiftly to ensure their families didn't end up involved. They now knew how dirty Thaddeus's crew were willing to play. The officer's hand hovered over the magnum that was holstered on his right hip. Nicky and Tony stood back, feeling completely powerless.

'OK, we get the message, now get the fuck off my driveway!' Tony snarled. He looked at Nicky, with his clenched fist and tightened cheek muscles. The seconds ticked away as the car reversed through the open gate and back onto Fletchers Avenue. They made their way into Tony's house through the side door, which led into the kitchen. Tony tossed the holdall onto the kitchen floor and punched the countertop without saying a word. Nicky was breathing heavily, his face grimacing with anger and fear.

'The fucking bastard ... this can't go on for

much longer!' said Nicky, tightening his clenched fists. The men's anger was immediately subdued when Nicky's phone rang. 'It's Marianna,' he said.

He cleared his throat and took a deep breath, before answering with 'Hi babe ... you all right?' Whilst Tony couldn't hear what she was saying, he knew she'd got Nicky's attention because he zoned in on what she was saying. 'Um .. umm ... OK babe. Yeah, OK.' The mostly one-sided conversation ended with, 'Thanks babe, see you later.' As Nicky ended the call, he looked up at Tony, smiling.

'Well, some good news for a change! Marianna's Bank's fraud department has handed over the counterfeit notes and the police have started their investigation. She said that the police will report back to her bank in seven days to give them information about their actions and the outcome!' Nicky paused and sighed. 'Well, at least we will have a result from this and the diamonds will arrive soon. If the police can link Thaddeus to the notes, it will be two issues sorted out in one go! If not, we'll have to go ahead with our original plans for him!'

'Well then, let's see what happens,' replied Tony, indignation still evident in his voice.

Nicky looked at his phone again. 'I'll just text Marianna and tell her that we are on a mission tonight and that I'm staying at yours.'

He continued, 'Teach, let's get something to eat and get our tools together. We can then rest for a while before we go and stake out Thaddeus's place. It might be a long night –we've never taken a trip up the river like this before!'

He paused as he looked at how distracted Tony still was; there were so many things going through his head. Mikey's murder, which they had both witnessed, and the fact that they were pretty much being framed for it, were encompassing his thoughts.

Even though the River Weather was much shallower from Tony's house onwards, neither of the men had ever walked or swum in it, so they had no idea how solid or how mushy the riverbed would be. Over the years, there would have been many fallen leaves and natural debris. They had no idea what kind of wildlife would be living in the mysterious water. As far as Tony was concerned, there could be a number of things hidden under the water's surface. Tonight would be their first chance to find out what was there and to determine how easy or difficult the approach to Thaddeus's house would be. No one would be able to see them – that was the most important thing of all.

It didn't matter whose house they were at. The two friends always made sure they had their own clothes at both places. They also had two mission ready-to-go bags, one at each house so that they never risked travelling their kits from one place to another, just in case they came across a police checkpoint or were subjected to a spot check. This meant that if anything came up, they were ready. They organised their wetsuits, military grade footwear, two makeshift knives, two flat waterproof flashlights, synchronised digital watches, and two old phones into two thick zip lock bags. When they were ready to go, their phones and flashlights would fit into a chest pocket and the makeshift corrugated steel knives would slide into open pockets just above their knees – on the right knee for Tony and on the left for Nicky – to suit their orientation perfectly.

They waited until nightfall before setting out; rather than risk losing his house keys in the river, Tony placed them underneath a broken flowerpot alongside other neglected and forlorn looking plants. Tony's garden reflected his non-attentive relationship with his family. His parents were mostly away enjoying their retirement and his other siblings had made lives for themselves elsewhere. Although the house was opulent, it didn't feel or look like a comfortable place to be. The outside free weight gym, with its crossbars and bow flex machines, was the only representation of recent activity. Oil that was used to lubricate the equipment was still dripping from its joints.

'Nicky, the keys are under here, just in case we get separated on our way back!' mumbled Tony, who was still feeling pretty angry from the incident with the police officer earlier. They knew the colour and design of Thaddeus's house from the front, but not from the back. They had no clue what kinds of trees or bushes would be at the back. It would take some guesswork to determine which house was his from the river. After learning what kind of person he is, Nicky guessed that Thaddeus would probably have installed barbed wire, or even an electric fence at the back of the property to make it difficult for anyone to get access to his land.

As they stepped from the bank of Tony's back garden into the temperate river water, Nicky felt dried branches snapping under his feet. The stillness and apparent depth of the water was deceptive as, after only a few steps, Tony was up to his waist in water.

'Shit! I wasn't expecting that at all! It's deeper than we thought, Nicky ... and much fucking colder too!!' Tony gasped and Nicky burst out laughing.

'You'll get used to it!' Nicky retorted, struggling to keep his balance as his left foot started sliding on some soft mud. 'I have no idea what we are doing! But we might as well keep going now we're wet. We've got two choices,' Nicky continued. 'We can stay in the middle where there's less debris, so we can wade through without getting our feet stuck or stay close to the bank and deal with the debris!'

Tony's chest was now under water. 'Either way, it won't be easy!!' he replied, shivering. 'We just need to get there and back the quickest way before we freeze to death. You decide. I'll follow you'.

Time was ebbing away; already three minutes had passed, and they had only moved about twelve metres up the river; they hadn't even managed to get as far as the next-door neighbour's fence. The depth of the water had prevented them from moving at reasonable pace.

'This is definitely not working!' Tony blurted out, as he swatted some kind of bug that had landed on his forehead.

'I agree with you, Teach ... totally ... this isn't working', Nicky replied. They were still only about thirty metres upriver and still had no clue where they were. They both agreed that the plan needed rethinking but decided that they would stay in the water a bit longer to see how far they could get, then they would be able to map out a path for their next attempt.

Looking at each for support, they both knew that using the river was the only way they'd be able to get to Thaddeus's house. They couldn't just drive to his house, because they would be seen. Neither could they stake him out from the front. Using a dingy might be a good idea but getting rid of the dingy after their mission would be a huge problem. They also had to be careful not to create an identifiable path from Tony's house to Thaddeus's place, as the police would be able to track them.

Nicky and Tony had been on many missions and had been unfazed by everything they had been faced with ... but they both knew that Thaddeus was the biggest beast they'd ever had to slay.

'Can you smell that!' Nicky whispered. 'Yeah, it would be difficult to miss it,' Tony replied. 'It must be some kind of dead animal!' Nicky muttered.

The embalming fluid smell same back to Tony and he screwed up his nose as he realised the smell here was similar. 'I guess so!' he replied, pointing his torch towards the riverbank. He looked at his watch. 'We have been in the water for forty-five minutes and thirty-two sec ...' Tony interrupted himself as he had to take a gasp of air.

'Wow ... that smell is really strong here!' his voice gave a squeak as he gasped for air again. They pointed their torches towards the riverbank and noticed tiny, circular lights reflecting back at them.

'Are they animals?' asked Nicky. 'I wonder what they are...' he continued. The two friends pointed their torches at the same spot and Tony took a step back in surprise as he saw the image of a small animal in the darkness.

'That's a cat ...' he said.

Nicky replied, 'There's more than one. Why are they not running away? I thought this would frighten them awa...' Nicky's voice petered out as the two men realised what they were looking at.

'Shit!' Tony gasped. 'What the fuck?!'

In front of them were about eight or nine cats, all dead and at different stages of decomposition. Their eyes were all open and staring out at the water. Nicky and Tony stared at each other in disbelief. They were both overcome with fear. Their hearts were racing and their bodies went hot and cold all at the same time.

It was an indescribable scene; the cats were hanging from the branches of the cedar trees on the riverbank. The ground was littered with the bones of other large animals and the stench was overpowering. Here, the water was discoloured because of the rotten flesh, infusing the water with a disgusting soup of despair. Whoever had done this was insane, demented and alien to common human values.

'I think we should move on!' said Nicky, looking at his watch again. 'I'd rather be away from this place.' They continued up the river noting trees and other identifiable features along the riverbank. They then noticed Rio Bridge, which connected Weatherpool to the neighbouring village of Churt. They realised they'd gone too far and must have already passed Thaddeus's house.

They decided to turn around and head back. After what they'd seen, their original plans would have to be ditched. They needed to think carefully as, whatever route they decided to take, they wouldn't be able to go back to Tony's after completing their mission. Only a few houses would have access from the river into their own gardens. They narrowed Thaddeus's backyard down to one within ten yards either side of where they saw the dead cat cemetery. However, they hadn't yet determined how they would get into any of the yards; Nicky had noted many steep inclines and ridges, with loose and unstable soil. In some places, there was no way of gaining a sufficient foothold.

An uncanny silence was broken only by the hooting of owls that watched the two men wading quietly back to Tony's yard. How were they going to overcome the obstacles in their path? As they climbed back up and into Tony's garden, they retraced their steps, retrieved the key, and opened the door. Relieved to be back safely, they stood in the kitchen and peeled their wetsuits from their frozen bodies.

With the first words that had been spoken since they climbed out of the water, Tony muttered, 'Well, that was something else!'

'I think we definitely underestimated what it's like upstream … I really didn't expect any of that!' replied Nicky, his teeth chattering.

'I can still smell the cats from here!' Tony laughed. 'What are we doing, Nicky?!' 'Nicky replied, shaking his head and chuckling to himself, 'I really don't know … What I do know is … I need a shower. A long one!'

He headed off down the passageway to the en-suite bathroom on the ground floor. Tony put his holdall next to the bedside table and walked towards the stairwell to his basement living quarters. He stopped as an overwhelming stench of embalming fluid again overpowered his senses. He descended the steps slowly, looking behind him as he did so.

Was his mind playing tricks or had Thaddeus been in here while they were wading upstream?

CHAPTER SEVEN

A long warm shower was exactly what they both needed to cleanse the experience from their minds and refresh their subconscious thoughts. Tony returned to the kitchen and found Nicky devouring a bowl of readymade noodles and holding a half empty bottle of lager.

'Um, sorry … couldn't wait Teach … that aquatic exercise made me so hungry!' He carried on eating for a couple of minutes, then continued, 'We need to be as fit as we can. Next time, we need to eat properly before we go!'

'I agree!' Tony replied as he turned towards the cupboard for a pot of noodles. Usually, he saw this as tasteless emergency food, but for some reason, watching Nicky eat, had made Tony fancy some too. As they ate, the two friends conducted a proper assessment of their situation; they recapped everything that they had endured during their reconnaissance. The two friends decided that they would take the same route again, but leave earlier, giving them the time to enter ten backyards before reaching the riverbank with the pet cemetery. After finding Thaddeus's dwelling, they would go back a third time for a detailed assessment marking times and routines, then a fourth and penultimate time to sequence and act out their plan. The two men knew the risks and they definitely couldn't afford to make any mistakes.

It had been an exhausting forty-eight hours and their bodies, especially Tony's, was yearning for rest and recovery. They bid each other good night and went to their separate rooms, the smell of embalming fluid still evident in the basement apartment, as if the Lucifer figure really had visited the apartment, if not in person, in spirit.

The next day, the sun had not long passed overhead, and the midday rays shone intensely onto the forecourt and dying flora and fauna. Nicky and Tony had to make sure they felt more physically fit and mentally ready to pursue the mission before them. Starting the day as they often did, the two men embarked on a series of routine stretches and exercises in the side garden, from which they could see the front gate and the motorbike parked on the forecourt. They knew that they required leg strength to wade upstream, speed and focus, and upper body strength. They had just started a workout that was as brutal as they had time for, when they saw Chandler's car pulling up at the closed automatic gate.

'Shit, I wonder what the bastard wants now!' Easing back the leg press and dismounting the bench, Tony got up and set off towards the gate. As he got closer, he could see that the policeman was accompanied by another male sitting in the front passenger seat. Before Tony got to the gate, the man got out of the car and walked towards Tony, leaving the passenger door open.

'The boss said that you should pick up the

money at Darren's workshop and bring it all to the strip club in Bramshill in two hours ... don't forget the diamonds, or you'll both be fucking dead!'

Before Tony could respond, the man got back in the car and closed the door. 'Hey, Hey!!' he shouted as the car drove off.

'What the fuck, man?!' Tony shouted, exasperated. He wiped away the sweat that had built up during his exercise as he contemplated the potential outcome of meeting Thaddeus at his strip club. They had lost all authority and the benefits from their endeavours would all go to Thaddeus. By now, Nicky had reached the gate. 'What did he say?' Nicky asked, perspiration also pouring down his forehead.

'I don't even know who he was!' Tony replied. 'But he said that we must get the money for the Brinks job that your Uncle Darren is holding for us at Free Port and bring it to the strip club; we have two hours!' He paused to catch his breath, 'In light of everything, we have two choices – disobey this guy or become one of Thaddeus's lapdogs and carry out his orders!'

'I know what you mean, Teach!' Nicky stuttered. 'One thing for sure is if we give him the money, they won't need us for the Brinks heist! So, let's not give it to them! They can't get rid of the diamonds without us either. We are the only ones who know the contacts in Watchmead Gardens ... no one else will buy uncertified diamonds!' Nicky's cheeks tightened. 'Let's get dressed and go and see them at the club.'

With sweat still flowing down their backs, the two men rushed into the house leaving the free weights strewn in the yard. The strip club was located approximately two kilometres northwest of Weatherpool in a town called Bramshill. The journey would take them past Thaddeus's dwelling, over Rio bridge, and then on a short drive through Churt before reaching the small opulent town. The Bells and Bottoms strip club was a converted bar with a thatched roof and stone walls, which gave it a modest look from the outside. Its interior had a blend of Contemporary and Bohemian décor and its girls were a fine mixture of provocative beauty and piteousness. They wore nothing but cocaine-induced smiles and underwear the size of a duck's feather.

This club was better than its rival, the Ram-Shack Mill. Even though Nicky and Tony had never been against pillow talk with women they didn't know, they had never ventured into any of the local strip clubs because they knew they were owned by Thaddeus. They also knew that the clubs had illustrious reputations for enchaining men, who, through their own curiosity, had strayed in off the quiet street.

Ten minutes after setting off, the oversized rubber wheels of the motorbikes skidded of the into the Bells and Bottoms car park. Looking dishevelled and anxious, they foraged for free bays to park in amongst the prestigious vehicles, most of which had documents and other items littered on the dashboard and front passenger seats, representing their occupants' enthusiastic departures.

Tony took the lead and walked toward the club's main entrance door; he was still sweating and trying hard to compose himself. He didn't want to look as nervous as he actually felt. He knew that their lives were at stake and there was a possibility that their families could be drawn into their spirals of misadventure. At the main entrance stood two women wearing see-through red and black laced lingerie. They opened the brown pine doors, which hovered one centimetre above the stone-paved landing that led to the dimly lit bohemian setting with its mahogany floor.

The blue and red stage lights darted across the metal poles anchored onto wooden barrels, which were placed strategically throughout the club. The male onlookers were captivated by the posture of the girl on stage, who was only wearing a feather look underwear. Nicky followed him as they weaved through the sea of drooling men and arrived at the bar where the police officer and the man who appeared at Tony's gateway were both seated.

'So, you're here!' said the officer, looking at them briefly before continuing to look intensely at the acrobatic girl on the pole.

'Yeah, we're here!' said Tony, 'But we didn't bring the stuff. We want to speak to Thaddeus.'

'Umm!' the policeman's glanced at them with disdain, then averted his gaze back to the girl on the stage. 'The boss is over there!' He pointed to the left of the bar without changing his focus. Thaddeus was seated with Kwame and another smartly dressed male who was hugging a black leather briefcase. The three seemed to be having a private show; the area in which they were seated was cordoned off and a girl faced them, moving her body around a silver pole in time to the music.

Nicky and Tony glanced at each other as they walked apprehensively towards the area where the stunning pole dancer was performing. Her left leg was stretched parallel with the pole, whilst her right leg was anchored to the top of a wooden barrel. Her pose opened many possibilities in the men's imagination.

'Yo, yo!' The grunt of the Satanic beast's voice pricked their attention.

As Tony was dumbfounded by the lap dancer's moves, Nicky replied 'We need to talk.'

'About what?!' grunted Thaddeus.

'Well, you see …', started Nicky. 'The stones haven't arrived yet … there seems to be a delay and I have checked with the courier company and they should be here in another two days or so'. He paused swallowing the stress that was paralysing his mouth. He composed himself and continued, '... the other stuff is with my Uncle Darren and we believe that's the safest place ... it would be mindless to move it here!'

Thaddeus stood up and walked towards the two friends. His imposing structure blocked out the stage lights and cast a huge shadow over them. The overpowering smell of embalming fluid numbed their fear. With the back of his left hand, he swatted Nicky off his feet, who knocked over a chair as he landed back-side first, before hitting his head against a wooden post. Tony felt weightless as he was then hoisted off his feet by his neck and thrown onto the stage, his body crashing into the barrel on which the performer was dancing. Dazed and semiconscious, and with Thaddeus's palm still cuffing his neck, he could hear the beast of a man telling the dancer to come over and sit on his chest. Tony's eyes flittered in fear as her posterior rested on Tony's torso. She smiled at the cheering crowd whilst rubbing her bottom up against his chin. He could feel the strength of Thaddeus's grip around his neck, blocking off his airways. The girl eased up as another girl came forward with a blade and cut off her underwear, exposing her waxed vulva and clitoris. As Tony passed out, he felt a warm liquid gushing over his face and chest while the excited laughter and cheering from the audience rang in his ears.

Tony had no idea how long he was out for, but Thaddeus had yet again displayed his fury for all to see; the two other girls and men who were with Thaddeus had continued watching the sole dancer perform and were still sitting in the same position. They must have become accustomed to Thaddeus's displays of force. Nicky was still on the ground and the other paying patrons, who were watching the other dancers, were in a trance and weren't paying much attention to anything else.

As he regained consciousness, a revolting smell of urine stifled him. He now realised what the warm liquid was that was soaking him to the skin. 'Get off the stage!' shouted Thaddeus. 'Make sure you have the stones the next time I see you!' Tony looked around as he scrambled to his feet, and slipped off the stage, leaving the puddle behind him. Nicky held onto the wooden post as he pulled himself to his feet. The two men looked towards the exit, then at each other, and hurriedly left; they passed the two hostesses and saddled their motorbikes. The dancer's liquor-infused urine was still running down Tony's skin and his shirt was soaked from the foul liquid.

Tony was lost for words as he revved the motorbike's engine and spat out a mouthful of urine and saliva; he removed his shirt, tossing it into a nearby industrial sized bin. The two men didn't say a word to each other on the way back to Tony's house. The journey felt much longer than usual but riding the bikes at speed help to create a sterilising effect as the harsh wind brushed against Tony's naked wet skin.

They arrived at Tony's house and rode their bikes between the opening automatic gates onto the driveway before uttering a word to each other.

'That was awful, Teach!' Nicky paused 'He is one disgusting son of a bitch. We've never been in this position. Never! It's got to end soon, but I don't see how!' he said.

'It needs sorting', said Tony. 'Let's find where this motherfucker lives and get this done!' It was now late afternoon; the bikes kickstands went down on the paved forecourt and the two men walked past the side door, potted plants, and the strewn weights before arriving at the riverbank at the back of the garden. They were more revved up than their motorbikes were, just a few minutes ago; the adrenaline showed through the pulped veins on their foreheads. Now that Tony was without a shirt, he removed his shoes, socks and trousers, keeping on his underwear. The soothing feel of the water against his urine-soaked body help to relax the tension that had been mounting since his return from Kinboasi. Nicky soon followed him into the water intending to find the house of the satanic figure that had caused them so much grief.

Without clothing, they waded through the water so much quicker and with much less effort. With the presence of daylight, they could see some features of the houses, making it easier to identify where they were. By now they had arrived at a house that was six doors away from the property with the cat cemetery. They decided to get out from the river and examine the back gardens to confirm which house belonged to Thaddeus.

'Definitely not this one!' Nicky shucked, 'but at least we know where we are!' He continued, 'This is the house with the elderly couple, Mildred and Fitzroy.' He rubbed his top lip. 'So, I believe we are about four houses away. We need to skip the vacant plot of land before we get there. Let's go back into the water and keeping going until we get to that point, then we'll only be two houses from the target.'

'I agree, at that point we can stay on land and walk ...' Tony said, swatting a bug that had landed on his left cheek.

As they got out and started to walk on the riverbank, they noticed they were making deep footprints in the mud. They stopped to look around at the objects around them ... they needed to find a way to cover their tracks ... maybe they could use something that could be disposed of easily and that would blend in with what was already around them. 'Look', said Nicky, pointing to a pile of rubbish. 'There are plastic bottles and bags there that we could use. A few of them are big enough to put our feet into... then we could kick them off and no one would know we'd been here.

'Good plan,' replied Tony. 'We should be at his house in less than a minute ... we can take them off when we get to his house ... slip them back on as we leave ... then kick them off on the riverbank when we get back in the water.'

'Brilliant,' replied his friend. 'Let's pile more leaves and dirt on the rubbish. Then, on the day, we can just blend in whatever we have used with the pile and head off.'

They crept through the bushes, trampling dried leaves and wildflowers, creating their own path until they arrived at the yard with the dead cats. Peering through the shrubs, they could see one of Thaddeus's cars and some clothes pegged out on the line ... and again, there was an unmistakable stench of embalming fluid. They stopped, crouched, then stretched out flat in a sniper-like posture.

'What do you reckon?' Tony whispered. Do we wait until he gets home or go back?'

Nicky was staring at the house intently. 'We should go back ... I don't think that we are ready for an all-night mission right now. We should prepare ... we don't want to be hungry and we haven't got anything to help us defend ourselves.' Nicky the pragmatist is often right.

'You're right,' replied Tony, realising how stupid he'd been to even think about going into Thaddeus's house half naked and with no backpack.

Looking around before they left, they noticed ritualistic objects dangling from tree branches in the garden, as if they were being displayed. There was a jerry-built alter, a stone's throw from where they stood, and the skulls of dead animals negotiated their place amongst decomposed tails and feet. The eerie feeling of death took Tony back to his childhood and the memories of seeing the bloodstained mirror in his neighbour's garden that terrible morning.

They retraced their steps to the river, carried out their plan with the rubbish pile, and quietly waded back to Tony's backyard. They were silent as they digested the gravity of the tasks ahead of them. Tony closed his eyes and sighed, as the humiliation of the incident with the pole dancer returned to his mind. They picked up their clothes and Nicky put his on. As Tony headed towards the house for something fresh to wear. 'I need to go and see Marianna', said Nicky. 'I'll catch up with my Uncle Darren too and find out what's happening with those counterfeit notes.' 'OK mate,' Tony replied as his friend proceeded to the driveway. Tony made his way into the kitchen of his family home and headed straight to the fridge for a cold cider. Entering the hallway to the basement apartment, he could feel the vibration of motorbike's engine and powerful exhaust as it exited the driveway above. Again, an overwhelming smell of embalming fluid lingered in the apartment; the scent cut into Tony's throat like a sharp knife. It wasn't just a smell … it was a presence and he could almost feel it scraping against his skin as he descended the stairs into the basement. 'This can't be my imagination!' he muttered to himself.

With a final gulp of cider before slumping onto the velvety sofa, Tony tried to block out the humiliation of the day by turning on the television and flicking through the channels. Just as his eyes were drooping with exhaustion, a voice shouted the words I CAN SEE DEAD PEOPLE!' His heart jumped as he opened his eyes in shock, realising it had come from the television. With a deep sigh, he fell back into a deep sleep full of the grave sights and foul smells of the day.

The next morning, Tony was still stretched out on the sofa, his phone still in his pocket. He realised that its pinging and vibrating was what had woken him up.

Daylight beamed through the skylight roof in the basement apartment. Tony got up from the sofa and stood at the window; he could see several black tussock caterpillars crawling across the wet lawn. He recalled seeing those type caterpillars a long time ago; they reminded him of his childhood and days when he and one his brothers, David would play in the backyard, looking for and capturing these curious looking caterpillars. They pretended they were aliens. Even as they got much older David, Nicky and Tony still continue looking for the tussock caterpillars, as if they hadn't aged, stuck in the past at age nine.

He took his phone out of his pocket and looked through the notifications. There were no messages from Nicky, which was very strange, but he had a message from Kwame stating that they needed to book flights again to Sanibo, so that they can revisit Kinboasi. It seemed that he was also tracking the arrival of the laptops with the diamonds; he must have been, because he knew they were supposed to be arriving today. At that moment, another notification chimed from the delivery company, stating that the laptops would be arriving between twelve noon and one pm. It was going to be another hectic day.

Tony forwarded Kwame's message to Nicky as he walked up the stairwell to the kitchen. Tony expected an instant response, but there were no reply. It was unusual for him not to hear from Nicky for such a long time. Even though they had been best friends since primary school, Tony had begun to doubt Nicky's sincerity after leaving the hospital. He seemed to become more reserved and secretive, and Tony couldn't ignore the fact that an unmistakable and familiar odour was accompanying his friend. He decided not to think too much about it.

The kitchen curtains at the sink were open and, leaning forward, Tony could see more caterpillars crawling on the window above the kitchen sink. Another odd and unexplained occurrence that required investigation! He walked over to the pinewood side door. As he pulled it open towards him, he heard the musical plopping sounds of black tussock caterpillars as they fell to the floor. He jumped back in shock and awe and his eyes widened in surprise.

'What the f....!' he shouted.

There were hundreds of tussocks still hanging on the door and at least fifty had fallen onto the floor. He placed his feet carefully between the scattering of caterpillars on the floor and made his way through the open door and onto the landing in the backyard. He turned around to look at the back wall of the house ... the caterpillars had covered the entire wall; their movements create a wavelike motion, which coincided with an overwhelming stench of excrement. The combination resulted in Tony heaving uncontrollably. He attempted to understand what he was seeing and wondered how on earth there could be thousands of caterpillars covering his house wall. Tony rushed back through the side door and into the house, trampling whatever was on the floor in front of him. He went straight to the broom cupboard for a pan and brush and began to sweep away those that were on the kitchen floor. The scent of embalming fluid now overpowered by the acrid stench of the tussocks. He slammed the door furiously as he tossed out the last pill of caterpillars on the dustpan. 'This is unbelievable! Where did they all come from in such a short period of time ... pretty much overnight' he said to himself. 'They must have been breeding somewhere in our gardens!' He pondered as they crawled across the window and then decided to take a photo of them and send it to Nicky.

He wrote, 'I guess I need to contact the pest control company.' Again, he didn't get a response from his message to Nicky, so he decided to have a shower to cleanse his mind and body from another unpleasant experience. As he head to the shower he dial the number to a local pest control company. If Tony was superstitious, he would have believed what the West Africans had said about the mythical properties of diamonds. Their belief is that blood must be shed and donated to the spirits who are to look after the earth's minerals; we cannot simply take the minerals and not give something back. So if that is anything to go by, Tony considered if he'd been cursed for not giving blood back to the earth in Kinboasi, from where they had taken the diamonds. It felt as if the pressures of the world were weighing down on him and on all the plans that the friends had been working on, were falling apart. Tony was in the shower, when he heard the gate's intercom ringing. Tony quickly got out of the shower, slipping on some flip-flops and grabbed his robe as he ran up the stairs to speak to whoever was at the gate.

'Hello ... Hello?' Tony gasped. 'How can I help?'

There was no answer. He tried again ... 'Hel...', but this time Tony's stuttering was interrupted by a female voice. 'I've got a delivery for this address ...!'

'Thanks, I will be out shortly!' He paused to make himself more presentable then exited the side door, where the hordes of tussocks still dangled from the wall. He blocked his nose and proceeded to the gate where the courier van and delivery driver stood.

Tony opened the automatic gate and collected and signed for the packages containing the laptops. The driver apologised for the delay in delivering the items and explained that some of the packages, including his, had to go through extra checks to ensure that they were safe to enter the country. She noted on her clipboard that the laptops were fine and bid him farewell.

This was really significant. They had successfully smuggled diamonds out of West Africa! It wasn't just a few carats – they'd smuggled approximately two hundred carats worth between one hundred and seventy-five thousand United States Dollars to three hundred and fifty thousand USD in cash. Their smuggling system was simple yet sophisticated and needed a very low investment for a high return. What a pity that the two friends wouldn't benefit from the project in any way (apart from staying alive). Thaddeus made it clear that they would be forced to hand it all over to him. They would also have to take him to their trading contacts in Watchmead Garden, the only professionals in the business willing to pay cash for such treasures. Thaddeus would have gained their entire fortune and the tools with which to benefit from smuggling diamonds again and again. They would be completely dispensable and that was dangerous; there was no way that Tony was going to let that happen.

On receiving the packages, Tony was so enthusiastic about the delivery that he forgot about the caterpillars. He gleefully walked into the kitchen and closed the door behind him. He placed both packages on the kitchen counter, freeing his hands to check his phone to see if Nicky had replied, but he hadn't. For a moment, he considered messaging Marianna to find out where he was, but he decided it was best not to, in case he'd told her he was at Tony's. The joys of the murky world of deception.

The packages were in pristine condition; looking the same as they did, when they were handed over to the courier in Kinboasi. Tony grabbed a knife from the drawer and carefully slit the security sealing tape, then opened the first box to reveal the inner padding that had protected the laptops. The first was in mint condition; he carefully removed the laptop, then the disguised batteries. As he opened the fake end of the first battery, the precious stones sparkle as they sprinkled gently onto the countertop. Gathering them carefully into a little pile, he repeated the same steps for the second laptop and batteries. He counted them; altogether there were twelve. Ten smaller diamonds and two beautiful larger stones. That was a substantial number – their first attempt at smuggling diamonds had worked! This would be the start of something amazing. Nicky and Tony just needed to get rid of Thaddeus and make this smuggling business their own, which is how it was when they first put their plan together. Tony was not going to let anyone take this away from them. He stared at the glittering nuggets of compressed carbon and his phone, which lay next to them, wishing that Nicky would reply to the messages that he'd sent him; he checked but there was still no response.

The gate intercom rang for a second time of the day; this time it was pest control. Tony took a zip-lock sandwich bag out of the kitchen drawer and scooped the diamonds into it; sealed it and stuffed it into his jeans pocket. He opened the gate to allow the van onto the driveway. As he approached, Tony could see the look of astonishment on the driver's face.

'What's happened here?' He looked at the house, gloomily. 'This is going to be a big job. Do you know where they came from? I mean ... the source?' He lifted his phone and started to take pictures of the house that was now blanketed with hordes of black and red caterpillars.

'I have no idea!' replied Tony, his right hand in his pocket, clutching the bag of precious stones. 'That's why I called you ... you're meant to be the expert!' Tony continued, 'I woke up this morning to see exactly what you're seeing now!'

The pest control operative was quiet. Tony interrupted his thoughts by demanding, 'Well!? Can you sort this out or do I need to call another company!?'

'S-sorry Sir...!' he stuttered. 'Yes I can, but I will need another colleague's help ... I've never seen so many of these caterpillars in one place. For sure there is a source but they must be attracted to the walls of your house because of a smell or taste.' The man stopped talking and started looking around him.

'So, there's something on the wall?!' asked Tony, impatiently.

'There must be!' the man replied.

'Ok!' Tony retorted. 'Well ... I have an appointment so I will have to leave you to get this sorted. I gave your office my bank card details. I don't care about the cost, just get rid of them!'

Tony hurried back to the kitchen and then to basement apartment to get dressed and to pick up the keys for the motorbike. He wanted to make sure that he got to the strip club before the traffic started to build during the rush hour. The pest control operative's head was buried in the back of his van as he unpacked the equipment he needed to eradicate the caterpillars. He didn't notice the speed at which Tony raced out of the driveway and down Fletcher Avenue. As Tony picked up speed, he rubbed his right elbow against the lump in his pocket, just for reassurance.

He arrived at the club and made his way past the girls at the entrance, stepping in to the dark, oppressive interior of Bells and Bottoms. He walked straight towards the area that they'd met Thaddeus on their last visit. As he got closer, he stopped in total disbelief.

'Seriously? Nicky?' he growled to himself. 'Am I seeing straight?' he rubbed his eyes and shook his head, looking up again to find Nicky sitting next to Kwame at the table with Thaddeus and four of the dancers, including, the one who had urinated all over him.

'For fuck's sake, Nicky... what are you playing at?!' he muttered to himself. Taking in a deep breath, he started walking towards the group again.

He approached the table highly suspicious of the only true friend he had ever known. The questions stampeded through an avalanche of thoughts. He took in the cosy body language being displayed by everyone at the table. Nicky's head, which was nestled on the chest of one of the women, raised as Tony arrived at the table. His glossy eyes looked up at him without emotion nor expression. It was as if Tony was looking at a stranger.

'Hey, Teach!' slurred Nicky.' Sorry, mate ... I forgot to call you and tell you so come to the club!' He looked at the half empty glass in front of him.

'Plus I got distracted by these beautiful ladies!' He looked towards the breasts of the dancer on whom he was leaning. Tony's thoughts were indescribable; it was now clear that he had to consider getting rid of Nicky after their plans to kill Thaddeus had been executed. He could even be walking into a trap right now.

Nevertheless, he kept his composure and replied, ' I thought something had happened to you. You didn't pick up my calls or reply to the messages I'd sent.'

'Sorry, Teach ... I don't even know where my phone is!' Nicky stuttered, trying to lift himself upright on the seat to look for his phone.

'Never mind ... it's not a big deal!' he replied and then, thoughtfully, continued, 'I have the stuff from West Africa... you know...'

Thaddeus and Kwame looked at Tony. 'What do you mean?' barked Thaddeus. 'TALK PLAIN'.

'I mean I have the stones!' Tony's quaking voice replied. He pulled the zip-lock bag from his jeans pocket and placed it gently on the table in front of them.

Kwame looked at Lucifer and exclaimed, 'I told you that these boys would deliver!' he laughed out loud, touching the bag of diamonds. As they moved the bag, the light glistened on the stones and it was clear that the girls at the table were impressed. 'Are ... those ... diamonds?' Asked one of the dancers, complete in awe.

'Yes!' replied Kwame. 'These are what you'll be bringing back with you!' He paused, then continued, 'Well, not these ones exactly, but similar!'

Thaddeus looked on, as he took the bag and opened it. 'Kwame told me that the diamonds should be worth about half a million dollars?'

'These should be worth around three hundred thousand dollars, give or take.' They all looked on, at the stones and then gazed at Tony in awe, impressed with this new source of wealth.

Thaddeus reached out and took hold of the bag in one of his huge, rough hands. 'We cash them in today!' he demanded, hiccupping then letting out a huge belch for good measure.

'Ok. Sure.' Tony retained a cold blank expression as he felt Nicky's stare. His suspicion heightened as he realised what could lie ahead. Nicky was not the same person that he'd called a brother and best friend for most of his life. His 'friend' was keeping something from him.

Selling the rough diamonds would be straightforward, much easier than smuggling them out of Africa. It is often thought that smuggled diamonds – most of which are considered to be blood diamonds – are kept out of formal trade and don't form part of the mix within the jewellery industry. Well this is a false truth because most diamond dealers make higher profits from mixing smuggled uncertified diamonds with Kimberly Certified diamonds. They pay much less for the uncertified ones and cover their unlawful purchases of such items by classing them as jewellery. They then cut the rough stones and blend them with other stones to create authentic jewellery.

Over the years Nicky and Tony had met several jewellers in the diamond district of

Watchmead Gardens, some of whom were willing to pay cash for uncertified stones, including rubies and diamonds up to a value of three million dollars. Whilst they had never had the opportunity to sell those jewellers the rough diamonds, they had kept in touch with them, visiting their offices whenever they were in the area and had sold items they'd picked while undertaking small jobs, such as the one they undertook at the Saunders'.

The security systems employed at the jewellery offices comprised a range of high and low levels of technology. Their favourite jeweller was Mr Sheikh. His office was located in the basement of a multi-storey building. Access could only be gained via a small elevator, which only held two people at a time. At the entrance door, a South Asian girl was paid to vet potential customers who approached the building. If all seemed clear, the girl would take the customer into the building and to the lift. She would accompany one person to the basement office, returning to fetch others in a timely manner. After alighting from the elevator in the basement, the customer would proceed onto a corridor that took them to a security door. That door led into a small room one meter square, in which there was an intercom system accompanied by a camera. Customers would then be allowed into Mr Sheikh's office in pairs, but only after showing the camera the items they had brought to pawn or sell, or perhaps money with which they intended buying jewellery from him. Inside the office were usually four or five people: Mr Sheikh and Mr Sheikh senior, who was his father, and sometimes, Mr Sheikh's brother. If a large purchase was being dealt with, other business associates with their accompanying bodyguards would also be present.

The room had two desks with a single chair on either side, a jewellery display stand, a tan three-seater leather sofa, and five foot tall fortified wrought iron safe. There were weighing scales of various sizes and descriptions, magnifying glasses, microscopes, and other gauges and implements on the display stand and on the desks. The Sheikhs claimed that their safe contained three million dollars in cash on any given day. They were considered to be astute businesspeople; if there was a bargain to be had, they wouldn't miss the opportunity. If they saw something that made business sense they wouldn't allow the customer to leave without offering them a persuasive amount of money. To make a reasonable profit from their business dealings, they would buy rough or uncut stones – diamonds, rubies, various gemstones, and gold. They would then smuggle them to India, where they would be cut, shaped, made into jewellery and returned to their office ready for sale. All the pieces of jewellery in their offices were unique and were sold at a high price. From Thaddeus's strip club, the group of men would head to Mr Sheikh's office, confident that they would get a reasonable price for the stones. From the previous discussion and Thaddeus's threatening behaviour towards Nicky and Tony, the two friends understood that they would not be receiving any of the money from this diamond sale. What was even more concerning was that they were now also giving up their contact – Mr Sheikh.

Even in the darkness at the strip club, Tony could see that Nicky was unbalanced. He was avoiding eye contact with Tony and hadn't been close enough to him for their usual brotherly handshake. Something was REALLY off.

The group left the strip club in taxis, arrived at the Diamond district, meeting the girl, who vetted them and followed the protocols of entering the jewellery shop. The Sheikhs examined the stones and were very pleased with the quality of the diamonds and after some frantic negotiation they exchanged the stones for three hundred and seventy thousand dollars.

If the deal continued in this way, there would be no doubt that millions would be made over the following few months, and it could only get better when the girls were thrown into the mix.

CHAPTER EIGHT

'It's best if you two take the money...' said Nicky to Thaddeus and Kwame in an authoritative tone. 'Teach and I will make our way back on our own...'

Thaddeus looked at the oversized holdall packed with money next to the display stand. He said nothing but bent down and scooped up the bag, his biceps contracting with ridged veins protruding. One of Mr Sheikh's entourage stepped forward and opened the security door allowing Thaddeus and Kwame to walk free from the confines of the fortified office and onto the corridor from which they would enter the lift that would then lower them to the ground floor.

Nicky said nothing as they stood in the office allowing them to leave with the money.

'We should head back to yours!' said Nicky., turning to look at his friend. 'I will tell you everything I found out!' Tony looked at him blankly. Nicky repeated, 'I'll tell you everything, OK?' Tony looked away, without answering.

'Thanks gents!' he exclaimed, stepping forward to shake Mr Sheikh's hand to show his appreciation of the deal, even though he knew that they wouldn't benefit from it this time. Nicky followed suit, warmly thanking each of the men in the room. Tony told himself that the dynamics of the next diamond deal would certainly be different. Once they had given their thanks and after five minutes of small talk, they left the office, following the footstep of Lucifer and his sidekick, Kwame. The two friends stepped out onto the pavement and hailed a taxi to take them to Tony's house.

The two men got in and sat down. They sat opposite each other, Tony facing the rear, as he preferred to watch vehicles that were following. He looked at his so-called friend, who was avoiding his gaze, and tried to work out what was going on. Why was Nicky acting like this? He wondered how he would explain being all cosy with Thaddeus at Bells and Bottoms. Nicky looked over Tony's shoulder and ahead. This was almost a reflection of the way they had dealt with things that had happened to them during their lives. The impact of past events still lingered and amplified Tony's actions, but Nicky was different – he lived for now and the future and seemingly did not care about the past.

There was an definite bubble of tension in the taxi as they travelled, making the journey feel much longer than it actually was. As they got out of the taxi, Nicky suddenly broke his silence.

'I'm sorry for not keeping you in the loop, mate,' he said, apologetically. He explained that one of them needed to get closer to Thaddeus to see what he was doing and planning. He went on to say he didn't think that Tony was the right person for that task, so he'd nominated himself and believed it was the right thing to do. 'I'm glad I did it,' he said, then went on to explain what he had found out and that it would definitely help them.

Nicky continued explaining what he had discovered. 'Thaddeus carries out a ritual. He sacrifices a cat every ninth night at nine pm. He burns incense and bathes in embalming fluid. He believes that he can consume the life of a dying cat and make himself invincible.' Nicky laughed as he looked at Tony's gaping mouth. He continued, 'He calls it the nine-lives theory.'

Nicky looked at Tony intently, waiting for his reaction. His friend shook his head and said, 'That's a hell of a story ... a load of baloney, if you ask me!'

Nicky paused as he walked towards the side door of the house. He screwed up his nose and said, 'Shit, what's that smell?'

'I had my own drama!' Tony replied, laughing at his friend's face, all screwed up in disgust. Tony showed him the photos and explained what he discovered that morning.

The two men went into the kitchen and Nicky, gratefully, closed the door behind him. Tony went straight to the kitchen booze cupboard and took out a bottle of Hennessey whiskey. He poured two large measures – no ice, no mixers. Sitting together at the kitchen table, they talked about their next move. Upon hearing the story about Thaddeus's ritual, and discovering from further details from Nicky that the last ritual was nine days ago, Tony decided that they should go back into the river and follow the now familiar path to the cat cemetery. They downed another triple measure to numb their senses and got ready for their new mission. They needed to leave at half past eight to be there in time.

As they had done on a number of occasions now, they removed all of their clothes – apart from their underwear. They decided this time to apply a thick layer of petroleum jelly all over their bodies to protect them from the cold. They then collected the few items that they would need for their reconnaissance. The moon shone on the chrome weights, lighting up the backyard as they both drained their glasses for the third time. Nicky looked at his diving watch and said, 'We need to go. Ready?'

Tony nodded and leaving the key in the same spot as before, he felt the effects of the whiskey warming his insides and preparing him for what he was about to witness. The River Weather was still and the glow from the moon created an ideal atmosphere for such a ritual. Tony felt a mixture of dread and excitement.

Wading through the still dark waters for approximately fifteen minutes, they climbed onto the riverbank two plots away from their destination. They walked on the dried leaves and branches that took them to their previous vantage point; they would be able to hide there and get a full view of Thaddeus's demented worship. The two men said nothing to each other but looked around to make sure their presence wouldn't spook any wildlife that might live in the shrubs.

They lay still for twelve minutes, then at three minutes before nine o'clock. Thaddeus came out of his house, looked around, then went back inside. He came out again, thirty seconds later, carrying a brown wooden box. From a distance it seemed as if the box was either heavy or contained something fragile. He placed it delicately in front of what could only be described as a sacrificial alter. The two friends knew that they had no chances of attacking him from where they were. The distance was too far and they were positioned twenty or so metres to his right. He would easily see them coming. They needed to approach him from behind, and even then, they would only have seconds to execute him. That would put their vantage position at the edge of his garden almost opposite his backdoor. It also meant that they would need to take wire cutters to cut the fence and leave his garden at a different way to their point of entry.

Thaddeus's towering figure stood next to the altar, as he took various implements from the wooden box and place them on it. He was very focused as he gently place a wooden bowl, three small bottles of liquid, and three candles on the table. He moved the candles into position – one on either side of the bowl and the third in front of it. He reached into the box and pulled out three incense sticks; he put them into a small pot next to the candle on the left.

He stopped and stood back to look at the display on the alter. He stretched out his arms towards the altar to acknowledge it was complete. He then walked over to a small wooden shed, which was no taller than his waist and opened the latched door. Nicky and Tony couldn't see what was in the shed, but they suddenly heard cats meowing, which confirmed their fears. Thaddeus closed the shed and headed back to the house. The friends looked at each other without saying a word, their eyes aglow with fear and disgust, knowing what they were about to witness.

After what felt like twenty minutes, but was actually only two, the satanic beast alighted from the house. This time he was wearing only black underwear and tucked on his right hip and under his right arm was his one-year-old child. Tony's eyes widened, but Nicky dropped his head, shaking it slowly. Tony felt his pulse starting to race. There was just enough space for Thaddeus to sit the child on the altar, The alter had just enough space for Thaddeus sit the child down. He then took a match from the box and struck it against a stone brick structure, which stood next to the altar. Once lit, he proceeded to use the match to light the candles and incense sticks. Leaving the child sitting perilously on the edge of the table, the beast then went over to the shed, opening the door again to the sounds of the wailing felines. He reached in and pulled out a cat that had its hind and forelegs all tied together. Its struggle was futile, as Thaddeus was squeezing its neck aggressively. He walked over to the altar with the chocking cat and tossed it onto the table next to the child. The cat's cry turned in to a scream, as Thaddeus took a rusty looking blade from the box and quickly slayed it, with the child looking on, just centimetres away. There was an uncanny silence; the chirrups and chatter of the evening wildlife stopped. It was if that moment in time was being absorbed. He picked up the deceased cat and drained its blood in the wooden bowl on the altar.

Throughout this shocking ritual, the child just gazed at the candles with very wide eyes. He displayed no emotion. It was clear that this was not the first time the child had witnesses this activity.

Nicky's body was frozen in its crouched position; he clamped his teeth together in astonishment as Thaddeus drained the last few drops of blood into the bowl. Nicky looked round at Tony who was also transfixed as he watched Thaddeus adding drops of some kind of liquid from one of the bottles into the bowl. The two men both winced and looked away as the beast lifted the bowl to his mouth and, his face beaming with delight, drank some of the contents. Even more shockingly, he then put the bowl to his child's mouth and forced him to drink some of the blood.

'Fuck ...' said Tony quietly, shaking his head. Nicky placed a hand on Tony's back to steady him. Thaddeus continued with his chanting, fanning the smoke from the incense towards himself and the child. Throughout the ritual, which lasted for no more than ten minutes, Thaddeus was in a trancelike state; he was totally focused on the process. This would have been a perfect moment for Tony and Nicky to make their final move, but they were not in a position to do that today. They continued watching as Thaddeus attached a cord the cat's swollen neck and hanged it on a horizontal pole that rested above the altar. He picked up the child, walking backwards at first while he seemingly admired his work, then turned around and climbed the steps onto his back porch, then into the house.

The two men immediately moved from their positions and made their way back into the river. Their minds were racing as they waded back through the cold water. Their reconnaissance had been timely and they'd gathered substantive information that they could now act upon. Thaddeus performed this same ritual every nine days at the ninth hour. This gave the two men a timeframe to work to. They needed to convince Thaddeus and Kwame to make the next trip to Kinboasi, West Africa in eight days' time. The men knew that Thaddeus no longer needed them for the Brinks heist nor to sell the smuggled diamonds. The only thing he needed them to do was to go to Sanibo and Kinboasi with Kwame and the girls for the diamonds. If they didn't act fast, it wouldn't be long before he wouldn't need them for that either.

They moved silently through the last few metres of water towards Tony's back yard. The scenes of the ritual was playing over and over in their minds. What they'd just seen was insane! The man, Lucifer Thaddeus was mentally sick.

The next day, Nicky and Tony would return to Bells and Bottoms to set up their next trip to Sanibo and onto the village of Kinboasi. They knew it wouldn't be difficult to persuade Thaddeus, especially after the wealth he had just gained from their first smuggling trip. They just had to make sure that their flight date coincided with the ninth night after today's ritual. The trip to West Africa would be very different this time. They would be returning with diamonds of up to one thousand carats in total. These would be divided between the four girls, so each would be carrying two hundred and fifty carats. Nicky and Tony would travel together as they would have no chance in benefiting from the diamonds that the girls were carrying. They aimed to transport some diamonds for themselves using another method of concealment. For sure, they would find a way to carry the diamonds. In laptops again, maybe. Kwame could never find out about it.

After a perturbed night of sleep, Nicky and Tony got up with no urge for breakfast. Their stomachs were still affected by the gurgling sounds of the dying cat. Instead, they directed their adrenaline onto the outdoor gym and exercised hard. After, they quenched their thirst on another bottle of whiskey – a conflicting health choice, but a much needed boost. Once showered and dressed, they hopped into a taxi and asked the driver to take them to Bells and Bottoms, where they had left the motorbike and Merc the day before.

They alighted from the taxi just before noon and stood for a moment on the now familiar car park at the strip clubhouse; they looked over their vehicles, then walked past the two girls on the door, adorned with nipple tassels and feathered underwear. The club was already heaving with midday suits, briefcases, and neighbourly acquaintances seated in the areas closest to the stage. They acknowledged Chandler, the police officer, as they walked towards the left of the bar. They could see Thaddeus, Kwame, and a couple of the girls looking intently at a napkin on which the boss was drawing diagrams with labels. As he realised that the two friends were approaching, he picked up the napkin, scrunched it up into a ball, and stuffed it into his left pocket.

'So ... you guys are here! Welcome! You did very well yesterday, so today, we should celebrate and plan your next trip to West Africa!' He paused for a moment and then added, 'Guys ... just relax! You both look like you could eat a good meal!'

Thaddeus continued in a most unusual, almost charming, tone of voice. The prospect of making millions must have mellowed him. Tony also thought about the fact he had just performed his ritual too, so that could be another reason for being in a good mood. After all, being invincible would certainly be handy with all that cash to wallow in. For the first time, Thaddeus invited Tony to sit at his table. He then told the gals to put through a food order with oysters, calamari, hand-cut chips, whiskey, and cocktails and sparkling wines for the girls. The table was big enough to seat six people comfortably, but eight would be somewhat of a tight squeeze. Not that the dancers would mind; they knew there would a lap to sit on.

The bar tenders and waitresses scurried about to please their boss, deserting the other patrons in the process. The succulent oysters came on a huge platter, followed by whiskeys and the other listed items, delivered by waiting staff who donned panicked expressions but showed the utmost respect for the group. The mood at the table was very relaxed – the dancers jokingly took turns sitting on everyone's laps, twerking and dipping their bottoms as they rubbed themselves on the men's knees, hands, and other body parts.

Nicky initiated the conversation about going back to West Africa for more diamonds. Kwame reacted supportively and expanded on the notion.

They would need multiple visas for those going for the first time. Tony added that they would each need the yellow international medical book, to prevent the scenes at the airport that he had experienced. Tony still had not worked out, who exactly had played that joke of giving him a yellow pamphlet to take on his trip to Sanibo. Or was it a genuine mistake by Kwame? Thaddeus was less vocal to begin with, but he soon interjected, insisting that they would carry out test runs of various methods of bringing the diamonds back. They all involved the girls in one way or another, but it seemed that the standard method would be for them to swallow the diamonds. This would need to be tested beforehand to see how long they'd take to make their way out of the girls' digestive systems. Kwame mentioned the fact that they would have to be very careful the diamonds didn't 'arrive' before they'd left West Africa. At this thought, one of the dancers went extremely pale and cried out uncontrollably.

'Jess ... what's the matter?' asked Thaddeus, in a more gentle tone than any of the men had heard from him before.

'Nothing, boss!' she replied, weakly. She

picked up her cocktail and took the straw between her bright red lips to take a mouthful.

Out of nowhere, Thaddeus bellowed, 'LET'S GET THIS STRAIGHT, YOU FUCKING IDIOTS!'

Everyone around the table jumped at least an inch from their seats. The girl in question began to cry. Thaddeus took hold of her hair in his fist, aggressively. 'This is no pussy licking game ... I'm NOT ASKING you to do it ... I'M TELLING YOU TO DO IT!!!!' Breathing heavily, he paused and looked around the table staring at each and every one of his minions. Once more, he shouted , with some of the words directed into the face of the girl whose hair he was still gripping. 'GET OVER IT, YOU GOOD FOR NOTHIN' PIECES OF SHIT!!'

With that, he hammered his fist onto the wooden table and again, everyone jumped; it was as if court had been adjourned and the law had been laid. He let go of the girl's hair, and she turned to one of the other girls who comforted her. Thaddeus shook himself, his breathing starting to regulate. Apart from the sniffles coming from the girl, the group was silent.

'Umm ...' ventured Tony, leaning forward in his seat, 'I'm fine with that!'

Eager to get everyone to agree on a date that coincided with Thaddeus's ritual, Nicky was the next person to agree. 'Let's get this done!' he said, politely seconding Tony's proposal. 'Let's go next Friday; that's eight days from now!' He paused and took a sip from his glass. 'That will give us enough time to get the travel documents ready and book the flights.'

Kwame looking slightly tipsy, nodded his head in agreement. 'It means ... in ten days ... we could be back here with a ton of money, sexy women, and enjoying ourselves with a nice bottle of Remy Martin Louis XIII Cognac. What more could a man want!?' He burst into ill-fitting laughter.

'So, are we in agreement then?!' asked Nicky, looking intently at Thaddeus who was, at this point, staring into space. Kwame, still laughing, shouted, 'Why not? Why not...?' All of a sudden, he remembered himself and looked directly at Thaddeus, his face straight. 'What do you say boss?'

The group waited for a response. The silence

was eerie. The voice in Tony's head screamed 'Just say YES!'

Thaddeus took out his phone, opened his calendar, counted the days on his fingers and replied, 'Go in seven days, not eight.'

'Ok, boss!' Kwame replied. Nicky and Tony stared at each other in disbelief. On a positive note, they were going back to Sanibo Airport soon, but on the downside, they would be flying a day before Thaddeus performed his ritual. They knew that he would be at his most vulnerable during that time. They would have no chance of eliminating him before they travelled unless they could do it at that time. They now needed to consider their options carefully. They needed to slay the beast, Thaddeus.

Thaddeus took three small packets filled white power from his pocket. The sight of the angel dust set the girls' faces aglow. Even the whimpering girl stopped crying and looked up, eagerly. They licked their lips from side to side. Thaddeus certainly knew how to captivate his dancers and remove the stress and rough edges their work with him entailed. As he opened and poured the angel dust onto the wooden table, they looked on like hungry bears homing in on a salmon. Very politely, they took turns and showed upmost respect for each other. The closed one nostril with a finger and gracefully breathed the angel dust in like a gentle vacuum. This was not what Tony and Nicky were used to, but they were forced to pretend that they were enjoying what was on offer.

The dancers continued to indulge themselves at the table, whilst Nicky and Tony engaged Kwame in conversation. They talked about who would travel with whom, and when, and how. Kwame told them that Thaddeus has already agreed to pay the full cost of the trip, including the hotels, flights, and any other expenses. They agreed that the girls would stay at a hotel near the Sanibo airport, whilst the men would go straight to the village of Kinboasi to retrieve the diamonds. Kwame went on to say that in the coming week, would need to test systems of transportation, that is, the girls and where they would be putting the diamonds while travelling. One of his ideas was to insert the diamonds into tampons and insert them into the girls' vaginas. The only problem with that was the risk of losing them when they needed to use the loo. Another idea was for them to swallow the stones; this had been tried with drugs in the past, but it was both messy and smelly. Kwame didn't fancy that any more than Tony and Nicky.

Tony's science background kicked in and it came to him that they could cut meat and sew the diamonds into it, then put the meat inside the dancers' vagina. They could cut the meat so it was big enough to need someone with surgical equipment to remove it. It would be placed as deep inside the girls as possible. Nicky and Kwame both thought the idea was brilliant. They continued drinking and discussing flight dates and travel plans. Kwame would travel with the dancers to Sanibo, whilst Nicky and Tony would travel together, arriving a day later, which would give Kwame enough time to get the girls settled into the harsh African environment, and more importantly, give the two friends the opportunity to carry out their execution. However, on their return flights, Nicky would travel back with the girls and Thaddeus would pick them up at the airport. Kwame and Tony would then travel back a day later. The two friends agreed that they would pay for their own flights, but accepted Thaddeus's offer of footing the bill of the other expenses.

With that settled, the men continued to enjoy the frolics with the girls. Nicky and Tony kept glancing at each other, as if to communicate telepathically. They now knew that they could turn this horrific business back to their own advantage. They would smuggle the diamonds on their own once the devil had been slayed.

The daylight soon faded away, creating a more party-like atmosphere at the club. Thaddeus had elusively disappeared from the table. Tony gallivanted for a few more hours before bidding good night to Kwame, the gals, and Nicky. He'd had enough nipple licking for one night.

The days felt like months as they met day after day to plan the trip and get everything, including the girls, ready for the next smuggling trip. The first tests were to try out the obstetrical forceps and speculums with the dancers. We cut chunks of meat and inserted crystals inside it, making a few cotton stiches around it to secure them. The men observed the girls taking it in turns to lubricate the speculums before using them to open up each other's vaginas. They giggled and squealed throughout, which for the men, made the whole thing a bit of a turn on. The scene was almost pornographic. Tony told the girls to calm down before they starting practising using the forceps inside each other. A hospital visit was not on the cards – there was no time for that. It was a difficult scene to watch without the men feeling the blood rushing to their groins. As the girls calmed down, the men were in awe of how careful they were with each other's bodies. This was going to make them very wealthy indeed.

Amongst their extended list of things to do, the men spared no expense as they shopped and shipped suitcases with clothes and shoes, men's and women's underwear, laundry detergent, along with canned foods and rice. These were things that their contacts in Kinboasi told them were in short supply. They would also take along an extra iPhones and an iPad as they knew that those items would guarantee a positive response from the Chief and his villagers.

The latest flight that Nicky and Tony could get

to Sanibo was at half past eleven, which meant they had two and half hours to commit their murderous act. They talked about every detail – the timings, equipment, and routine to make sure they were ready for any eventuality.

The day arrived and everything was in place: Nicky and Tony went together to Belles and Bottom to see Kwame and the dancers set off to the airport and onwards to West Africa. The four dancers looked stunning. Tony's favourite was Jessica – blond with a body to die for and her eyes seemed to glow in the dark like one of the beast's cats. She was the one that had cried when Thaddeus lost his temper with her. His second favourite was Antonia – brunette, blue eyes, and one dress size up from Jessica, but nevertheless, stunning. Antonia was his nemesis, because she had been the one that had pissed all over him. The other two dancers, Tamara and Sasha, measured up to Antonia and Jessica but Tony found them too sexually provocative. They'd also snorted far too much angel dust over the years, and they couldn't tell the difference between reality and make-believe most of the time.

Kwame looked debonair, but stated that he

would be changing into some more local-styled attire once he had checked the girls into their hotel. As the party left for the airport, Nicky and Tony set off back to their own homes to prepare. At last, their time had come to take control of their destiny.

At twenty-five minutes to eight, Tony felt the vibration of Nicky's motorbike as he arrived at the automatic gate. He checked that everything was packed in his black and green rucksack, the same bag that had accompanied him on many ventures. This time it was going to be different, because they had never embarked on a technical mission that required so much precision. He made a quick sweep of the kitchen to make sure he'd left no evidence. With his backpack anchored to his shoulders, he exited the side door onto the garden, looking right at the weights in the outdoor gym and towards the backyard that led to the River Weather to acknowledge the finality of the task ahead.

'Come on, Teach!' shouted Nicky. 'We haven't got much time!

'I'm on my way,' he replied, shutting and locking the door behind him. Nicky looked militant.

He was dressed in a tight dark green t-shirt that showed all the ridges and curves of his biceps and torso. His black hair was waxed and tied back into a ponytail. The bottoms of his navy denim skinny jeans were tucked neatly into his dark green upper leather converse. The open face of his helmet complimented his appearance.

'You look ready for a date!' said Tony, smiling as he started up his motorbike and exited the automatic gate to join Nicky on his street, Fletchers Avenue . 'You don't look too shabby, yourself!' replied his friend, grinning as Tony tipped his bike sideways slightly and kicked out the stand. Tony revved the engine and the headlights illuminated the darkened asphalt as he set off after Nicky who had already sped off up the road and onto a myopic path that would have irreversible outcomes for them both in the future.

The rode their bikes in a synchronised fashion using a low throttle as they passed the neighbouring houses. After a few minutes, they rolled quietly passed Thaddeus's house. They continued until they reached the bridge that acted as a boundary between Weatherpool and the neighbouring town of

Churt. As they rode across the bridge, Nicky switched off his engine and went off-road onto a marl footpath that was generally used by fishermen to access the River Weather. Tony followed, copying his actions. The unpaved surface was hard against the oversized tyres, as the weeds brushed their legs and jolted against the tank. They had to keep their heads lowered, almost level with the bike fuel tanks in places, to avoid the low-hanging branches and vines.

After approximately one hundred and twenty metres along the path, they stopped, dismounted and pushed their motorbikes off the path and into waist high brambles. They removed two camouflaged bike covers from their backpacks to help disguise the bikes. There had been many stories of people disappearing from Weatherpool, so it would be unlikely that anyone but spirits would walk these paths after dark. However, the two men were not willing to take any chances.

They waited next to their bikes for ten minutes, just to be sure that no curious onlookers hadn't followed them down the path. They then prepared themselves. They took off all of their clothing, including underwear this time. They'd learned a lot whilst going out on their reconnaissance missions. They went lightweight and had no clothing or accessories that might slow them down or be left behind by accident. The last thing they needed was evidence against them. They just had to be really careful not to cut themselves or leave any body fluids behind.

They covered every area of their bodies with petroleum jelly. They then took one more handful of jelly each and Tony with his left and Nicky with his right, leaving their strongest arms to handle their makeshift corrugated steel daggers. They set off quietly and carefully down the path and towards the river, dodging low branches and avoiding skin snagging brambles on the ground. They reached the water and stepped in carefully holding one hand each above the water to keep the jelly dry. Instead of dragging their feet they took giant steps, placing each foot on the riverbed cautiously.

After ten minutes of taking long, fragile steps they spotted the glittering cat eyes between the branches of the trees. They looked at each other, and nodded, acknowledging that they would climb the neighbouring riverbank as they had done now on many occasions. As their feet stood firmly on the bank, they applied the rest of the petroleum jelly. This would provide enough lubrication in the event that Thaddeus might try to grab hold of one of them; covered in the jelly, they would be able to slip out of his grasp. It would also help them keep warm on the way back, if they made it that far.

They took their positions as before, ready to take the necessary savage action. Tony took deep breaths to calm his nerves. He saw Nicky's silhouette shaking with nerves. 'You OK, bro?' he whispered. Nicky nodded. Tony felt as if he was having an out of body experience. It felt to him like it was someone else doing this. Someone who was a demon and who was no better than Thaddeus.

A couple of feet in front of Tony, Nicky was contemplating the same. 'How did we get to this point?' he asked himself. 'What pushed us down this path of destruction?'

They had no timepieces with them but they knew that the real demon would be performing his ritual at nine. If all went to plan, that would give them twenty minutes to complete the mission and return to their bikes. It would be a mad rush to get dressed and drive their motorbikes to the airport. But they were more than capable motorcyclists and should be able to catch their flight to Sanibo, West Africa to meet Kwame and the girls as planned. No-one would be any wiser about their participation in the devil-figure's demise.

They crouched quietly, taking each breath slowly in and out to keep calm. Their breathing almost mimicked some of the sounds around them – the gentle breeze, the bats, and the crickets rubbing their legs together in the distance. Neither of them moved a millimetre; they just looked ahead and waited for the door to open and for Thaddeus to alight. The seconds felt like hours, but eventually, after approximately four minutes, their thoughts were interrupted by their prey and master, who barged through the kitchen door with his wooden box.

Tony's eyes rolled and his eyelids closed for just a second, as he summoned his inner beast that was required to complete this deed. They watched as he went to the shed and returned and slayed the cat. They had to walk in a straight line directly behind him so that the child didn't see them approaching either. They were aware that Marlena, the beast's wife, would have been somewhere in the house, probably somewhere that she couldn't see what he was doing.

They rose from their positions and made their way towards him. He lifted the bowl of blood and ointments and started to drink from it. They knew that he would fall into a trance and, at that very moment, they would strike. Thaddeus took a breath and started his first chant, which was grotesquely met by Nicky's corrugated steel beneath his lower right ribcage, followed by six ferocious stabs to his neck. Simultaneously, Tony's blade penetrated his left ribcage and armpit. His blood gushed from both sides, he twisted round and tried to lash out with an attempt at defiance; he didn't know which side to defend or attack. His huge hand hit Tony on the right side of his face and then his huge body hit the floor like a dead weight. His legs caught the altar, and the child fell down onto the concrete. As much as they didn't want to leave the child suffering like this, they had to go. The commotion would have woken the neighbours and would certainly have alerted Marlena.

The two men looked down at the beast, who, sprawled awkwardly on the ground, had stopped moving apart from the gushing of blood from his neck and side. To be sure that they had finished the job completely, they took a turn each at forcing their hilts into him one more time, straight through the upper torso and into his lungs.

Satisfied that the job was done, they slowly walked through the wooded backyard, then quickly onto the path from which they came. All of a sudden, the child was wailing and they heard the scream of a woman. They stepped back into the river and waded back towards their bikes. Before they got near enough to climb out, they both dived to the bottom of the riverbed and pushed their makeshift blades into it, pushing heavy limestones over them for good measure.

Although they were not quite out of the woods yet, they were relieved that they had overcome the fiend that had haunted them, and others, for far too long. They could now reset their sights on the dreams they had before the beast had got involved in their scheme. Tony's face was sore and his jaw ached from the slap that Thaddeus had managed to land on him, but he was satisfied that it would be the last punishment anyone was dealt by the hideous, evil man. The sight and smell of the man's blood had rekindled Tony's childhood nightmares; he remembered gazing at the bloodstained mirror that stood at the front of his murdered neighbour's house.

They eventually arrived at the edge of the bank and they climbed carefully onto the path that led back to the brambles. They hurried to their bikes and quickly pulled on their clothes. They weren't even wet; there was just, what felt like, a bit of sweat on their bodies as they rode their bikes at speed to the airport. They had executed their plan to near perfection. The rehearsals and reconnaissance missions had paid off. Now, they just needed to check in and fly off to new heights.

CHAPTER NINE

They left their motorbikes on the second level of the long-stay car park, covering them with the bike covers, as they had done on the footpath. Their check in, boarding, and take off went smoothly, but Tony had passed out before the flight took off, because he didn't remember fastening his seatbelt or ordering an inflight meal. When he awoke, there was a navy coloured blanket that had been place perfectly from his collar bone to his ankles. He rubbed his eyes, and on opening them, he also notice a meal of creamy salmon and broccoli pasta, with orange juice, on the tray in front of him.

He turned his head towards the aisle seat, and saw that Nicky had eaten his meal and drunk half of his juice. He had a pair of headphones on and was seemingly in a dream world.

'Hey bro ... how long was I asleep for?' said Tony in a groggy voice. He realised that Nicky hadn't heard him so he tapped him on the arm. This time, his friend took off the headphones. Tony repeated his question, his head pounding from the thump to the side of his head. 'I only remember getting onto the plane ... the rest is a blur.'

'All's good, Teach ... you should eat your meal.' Nicky paused pointing at the meal as he finished off his drink. 'We have two more hours before we land. Kwame will pick us up ... we'll head straight to the village as planned. We only have five days to take control of our life again.' He paused for a moment then continued, 'So far, we've made a bloody bold move towards that!' Tony smiled at Nicky's coded words, which were reassuring and measured. Nicky popped his headphones back on, looked around the plane as he nodded and jigged his head from side-to-side to what must have been an uplifting tune.

Tony relished the salmon and creamed pasta. Each mouthful melted away on his tongue. The smell of herbs and black pepper added mental stimulation that was needed after exerting a huge amount of force on Thaddeus. Even though the two friends had a lot going on in their minds, they said very little to each other during their last two hours on the plane. From time to time, they gazed at each other, smiling proudly about their accomplishment.

The cabin crew arrived next to them and took away their empty meal containers. Tony had purchased a duty free 100 ml Dior cologne for himself and a 50ml Armani for Keto, one of the Chief's sons. He and Tony had many conversations on his first visit. He was keen to leave his village to explore the wider world. His ideas were grand and Tony had promised him that he would help him achieve the goals that he'd set. In return, he would make extra effort to ensure that he would be well looked after when he stayed at Kinboasi..

Their overnight flight time ticked away and they had started their descent. Tony's previous experience with the immigration staff were still freshly etched in his memory, but this time he was prepared; he made sure that Nicky and the girls were ready too. Tony noticed that his friend was distracted by something. Whatever it was, he had chosen not to talk about it. Tony didn't like the fact that he was less talkative than usual; it made him somewhat suspicious.

Unlike his first experience at the West African airport, the immigration documentary checks were carried out without any issues. With their rucksacks on their shoulders, they walked through the airport lounge and were met by Kwame, who looked very serious.

'Hey, guys!' he called to them in a subdued voice. As they approached him and shook hands. 'You might want to sit down. it looks like you haven't heard. Thaddeus was attacked and he's in the hospital.'

'What?!' Nicky shouted, dropping his bag onto a lounge chair. He looked at Tony wide-eyed. Their eyes met and it was clear that they could not believe what they were hearing. How the hell was he still alive??

'Are you serious?' Tony said, looking back at

Kwame. 'What happened?' Nicky put his head in his hands wondering whether Thaddeus really was invincible and that his nine-lives rituals were paying off.

'The information I have is coming from the police sergeant. He seems to believe that Thaddeus was with some other people at the back of his house, practising voodoo, and something went wrong. It seems as though whoever he was with attacked him!' He paused shaking his head in an expression of horror. 'The people must have been really evil because even his baby son was injured! He's in hospital too!'

Kwame's tone calmed as he took a deep breath. 'Let's get out of here! We have to get on with the job, it's all up in the air now!'

As they walked through the exit, Kwame pointed to a taxi that seemed to be waiting for his return. 'This is our ride!' The driver was already seated and ready to go. Kwame sat in the front passenger seat, allowing Nicky and Tony to occupy the back seat. The car was much better than the car that had transported Tony on his first visit. The interior smelled fruity but there was no dirt or dust anywhere. The exterior was also a uniform yellow with a green stripe on each side. It looked like the same driver as before. He didn't introduce himself to the newcomers but spoke something in the local language to Kwame, who replied before they set off.

After hearing that Thaddeus had a chance of surviving, as low as it was, the two men needed to keep their ears to the ground and be ready to face the consequences if he did pull through and was able to give the police information about his attackers.

'So, Kwame!' started Nicky. 'In a worst case scenario ... God forbid that the boss doesn't make it ... what will happen on our return to Portland with the diamonds?'

Kwame hesitated and scratched his head, 'We have to carry on with the bosses plan as if nothing is wrong. We must return with the diamonds because he invested a lot of money in them. The girls are panicking because they depend on him for so many things!'

Nicky interjected, 'Maybe you could step into his shoes until he recovers? At least, that way, we all know where we stand and what the next steps are.' Nicky looked at Tony and nodded to get him to agree.

'Yep, that sounds like a good plan,' he said, looking back at Nicky. 'At least then there's some kind of continuity and you know a lot about the club and the girls.' He paused, then looking towards Kwame, he continued, 'We could work with you as you know the diamond business.'

Kwame looked out the window and then turned round to look at them both in the back of the car. He watched them for what felt like five minutes, but after just a few seconds, he said in a stern voice, 'I'll think about it ...' He continued to stare at the two friends for another few seconds, before turning back around and talking again with the taxi driver in a language the two friends could not understand; it seemed that everyone was calculating how much they could get for themselves, including Nicky. There was now a ghostly silence in the taxi; no one said anything; everyone peering blankly through their closed windows at the passing dew-covered banana and orange trees.

Much to Tony's relief, this time they didn't have to stop for any mechanical repairs; the car was in much better condition then the last one that he'd sat in and the journey took half as long. They arrived in lifeless Kinboasi. There seemed to be no movement, just the sounds of birds chirping and roosters giving their morning briefing.

Kwame broke the silence between the men. 'The Chief has arranged for us to stay at the same bed and breakfast as before. That's where we're going now. We can have something to eat and wait for the Chief to come and talk with us.' Nicky and Tony didn't reply.

There wasn't much of a conversation for the rest of the journey. The taxi arrived at the bed and breakfast and the men got out of the back and retrieved their backpacks from the boot. The driver got out and collected Kwame's two thirty-kilogram luggage and set them down at the entrance of the bed and breakfast. Kwame became angry with the driver, although Nicky and Tony couldn't understand what he was saying to him. The driver hastily picked up the bags and then stepped up to the door and entered the small lobby area, which also served as a bar, restaurant, and communal area. It was almost midday, groups of patrons and locals residents were actively participating in competitive feats of dominoes, checkers, and many were involved in boisterous debates. Kwame walked through the communal area to the bar counter, where he spoke to a member of staff. The staff opened a small black notebook, ran her finger down a list to find their names, then handed him some keys that were in an old plastic ice tub on the counter.

Kwame returned to where he left the Nicky, the driver and Tony standing and handed Nicky and Tony two sets of keys with different coloured tags; told them how to find their rooms. Tony's was on the left in the corridor opposite the bar. Nicky's was two doors down and Kwame's was the room beyond that. Kwame spoke again to the driver, who was still holding the two heavy bags. He handed his room key to the driver, who took the key in his mouth and shuffled away to deliver the bags to Kwame's room, wincing under their weight.

Looking around him, Tony noted that the hierarchy of respect here was odd. In most societies, young people are taught to respect their elders. But here, it seemed that respect was gained by an unknown factor. To us, Kwame was just an ordinary person just as we were, but to the locals here, he seemed to be someone who they should pander to. The two friends went to their rooms to deposit their bags and freshen up. As they entered the small corridor, they experienced the delectable fragrance of local food being prepared. Their hungry mouths began to water.

'Can you smell that?' Tony exclaimed. 'Whatever it is, I want some of it. I'm starving!'

Nicky smiled 'I'm willing to take the risk if you are.'

'We stayed here the last time', replied Tony. 'The food is quite good and their habits are pretty clean.' Pausing to open his door, he said as Nicky walked behind him towards his own room. 'You'll see. The server will provide bowl with water, soap, and towel for us to wash our hands before eating!'

'Really!' replied Nicky, as he unlocked his door further up the corridor. 'I need to dash, Teach I need the lav. See you in few minutes.' With that, Nicky was gone. Tony unlocked his own door, stepped into his room and closed the door behind him. He reached across to the wall in the dimly lit room and pressed a switch that turned on a very faint lightbulb attached to the wall. The emerald green room had a small window with blinds, a single wooden chair, a shower in the corner, enclosed by a curtain, a cream-coloured bucket, and red and green bed linen. Tony fumbled around the room, moving the chair from one end of the room to the other, to create some space. He looked at the sink and toilet, which was were in a separate rooms no bigger than a metre square. 'At least I don't have to use the bucket,' he murmured to himself.

Once Tony was satisfied that his room was as comfortable as it could be, he ventured out to the bar to finally enjoy the local delicacies that he could still smell coming from the kitchen. He entered the bar, observing Kwame and Nicky standing together, both with an open bottle of beer.

'Hey guys, sorry it took me so long!' Tony's chatter was met by blank stares as they contemplated something. His presence appeared unwelcome; how could this be? Tony and Nicky had been buddies for as long as he could remember. Kwame and Nicky continued to look across the bar as they took a mouthful of beer.

All of a sudden, as if jolted by a spear, Nicky said 'Hey, Teach! Sorry didn't see you there. We were just thinking about the girls and how we are going to execute our plans.' He paused and Kwame turned around to face Tony.

'Let's sit!' he said, looking as serious as ever.

Most of the tables were still occupied by men playing games or drinking. Kwame walked over to one of the tables, where two men were playing checkers, and said something to them. He then placed his bottle on the table. One of the men hastily picked up the board game, displacing the pieces from their positions; the other man stared at Kwame as though he had seen a ghost. They both got up and quickly walked away.

Tony's empty tummy was still yearning for the food that his salivary glands were expecting. Before sitting down with the others, he enquired with the bar tender what was being cooked in the kitchen.

The young man replied enthusiastically. 'At the moment they are preparing fufu, but we've already got fishcake made with yellow yam, spring onions, amaranth, and salted codfish. Also, we have crayfish soup with a mixture of root vegetables, okra and dumplings!'

Tony's taste buds were spoilt for choice, but he decided on a bowl of crayfish soup. He couldn't wait to experience the textures and flavours. The portion sizes were usually generous, so he knew that he'd be well fed. While he was busy with the bar tender, Nicky had made his way to the table with Kwame. Again, Tony was playing catch-up.

'Aren't you guys having something to eat?' Tony said as he arrived at the table.

'Not yet, I will stick with my drink for now,' replied Nicky, abruptly.

Kwame said nothing as he continued to drink from his bottle of beer. Tony had just sat down and pulled his chair under the table when his bowl of soup arrived. The server also placed an empty bowl on the table and asked Tony if he'd like to wash his hands. He accepted his offer, washed his hands in the water poured from a jug, and dried them with a cloth that was handed to him. The server cleared away the bowl that was used to catch the water and left Tony to eat.

'That smells and looks really good!' said Nicky. 'I might have that later.'

The server returned with an empty plate on which Tony could put any bones or shells from the soup.

'That's what I call service!' exclaimed Tony, smiling, as he took his first taste.

Their table fell silent as Tony slurped and cracked his way through the shells of the crawfish and ate its fleshy insides with great enjoyment. The coin sized dumplings were an absolute delight and soft okra melted as it landed on his tongue.

The silence was broken by Kwame's coarse voice. 'I have been thinking about what you guys said at the airport; about me taking over Thaddeus's business operations in Bramshill and Spanish Green!' He pause and took another drink. The two friends waited for him to continue. 'I don't actually need that kind of hassle. I'll explain,' he said, looking around.

'You might not know this, but most of the men in Kinboasi are former militia fighters, including me.'

He went on to tell them about the history of Kinboasi's and Sanibo's people and explained that he was a lieutenant in the local militia group. Their group had tried to take over, rule the country but, in the end, agreed a peaceful way forward. He said that he was responsible for the killing of many men and had killed a large number at first hand. His descriptions started to put Tony off his soup, so he put his spoon down and continued to listen. Kwame told the friends that most of the men in the village were part of that militia group. That explained why the men showed him respect and were fearful of him.

Kwame went on to say that if he killed anyone now, the local police would look the other way. He mentioned that while in the village, they must follow his instructions and do anything that they're told to do. He revealed that the Chief was a general in that militia group. Kwame explained that they would need to sacrifice some wildlife before taking the diamonds. He said that they hadn't made those sacrifices on their last visit and that he believed, it was for that reason Thaddeus has paid with his own life. If he was dead, of course. The group had not yet had any updated confirmation of Thaddeus's current condition.

Kwame continued to explain how he expected his companions to proceed. Listening to him, Tony started to think that they might have jumped from a frying pan into a raging furnace. His crayfish soup had suddenly become tasteless and cold, and his hunger had been replaced by an intense sense of survival. A thought flashed through his mind – what if they killed him too? But Kinboasi was HIS town, the people were on his side, so they wouldn't get away – not without help. Eyes and ears were everywhere, including the treetops and even where children played. Who would help and with what consequences?

Tony and Nicky gazed unemotionally at Kwame; they had seen many things and were thinking again on common ground. Tony hoped that Nicky was also calculating how they could get rid of him. That's if he was still on Tony's side? Kwame's ramble was suddenly interrupted by the booming voice of Chief.

'Sorry, I didn't see you there!' Kwame stood up suddenly. Tony followed suit, to demonstrate his gratitude. Nicky half hovered before returning to his seated position. As the Chief beckoned for a chair to be added to their table and sitting as it arrived, Tony noticed that most of the men had stopped their games and were showing reverence to the Chief. Keto stood behind him, demonstrating his own admiration to his Chief and father.

'I just came to say hello!' the Chief thundered. 'And I also wanted to say thank you for the many wonderful items that you sent to us! I will start distributing them tomorrow, but before I do, is there anything in the suitcases that belongs to any of you did you bring something special for someone?'

'It's all for you to do with as you wish!' Kwame replied. 'It's the least we can do for all the help that you are giving to us!'

'Thank you, that is most generous. The community will appreciate it all!' The Chief went on to tell us that Keto, his son, will accompany them whenever they visit the dealers to purchase the diamond. The chief said he was too busy as he had other local matters to deal with. Kwame introduced Nicky to the Chief has another associate and Tony's close friend. With a nod, the Chief bid the group farewell and exited the bar. Keto beckoned to one of the servers for a drink and sat down on the chair left vacant by the chief.

Keto sat next to Tony, with Kwame to his right and Nicky directly opposite. He shook Tony's hand warmly and offered the same to Nicky; he gave Kwame a brotherly hug and a handshake. Keto started by telling the group about new areas in which they'd found more diamonds and that they were of a wide range of colours and clarity. He echoed the Chief words about the gifts that had been brought for the villagers; he said that the community would really appreciate the clothes, shoes, bags, and food that we had given. He went on to say that it would certainly help to secure the best prices and the highest quality stones. Kwame did not mention the girls or the ways in which they planned to smuggle the stones. He just stated that they had a secure way to get the diamonds out of the country.

Kwame was keen to enjoy the company of local women as he had done previously, so he asked Keto to arrange a local woman for him for later. Nicky seemed distracted and disinterested in the conversation he nodded and grunted throughout the discussions. Kwame got up and said he was going to freshen up for his lady visitor. Whilst Nicky went to the bar for another beer, Keto and Tony were at the table alone. Tony took fifty dollars from his pocket and gave them to him. He had remembered that Keto said he often struggled to find enough money to look after his children. Tony said to him quietly, 'There's more ... wait here.'

Tony excused himself and quickly went to his room to retrieve the iPhone that he had brought for Keto. When he slipped back to the bar, Nicky wasn't there, but Keto's face was a picture as he saw what Tony was holding in his hand as he approached their table. He was like a child in a sweet shop and kept repeating 'Thanks, Teach ... this means a lot to me!'

Extremely pleased, Keto set off to organise a female guest for Kwame. With Nicky and Kwame busy elsewhere, Tony decided to retreat to his room to rest up for the busy and unpredictable days ahead. In the back of his mind he was still struggling to understand Nicky's mind-set. He had become reclusive and obscure, which worried Tony as this was not his usual personality. He hoped that the reason for his behaviour would come to light soon.

The night was long and Tony was unsettled due to the noise from the bar, the heat, and the various odours that kept emerging from the gaps under the door and through the open window. He awoke suddenly to the sound of bleating goats and chatter outside his room.

He looked at his watch with one eye. 'It's morning already??!' He felt compelled to get out of bed but had to disentangle himself from his bedding and the clothing he had left on his bed. He peered through the partly opened curtains and saw two hefty rams; there were also three cages with at least thirteen hens and, to the side, a Patas monkey tied by its neck with a rope. It was defiantly jumping onto the bark of the breadfruit tree and kept throwing itself at the cages of birds. The sound was deafening.

'What a commotion!' Tony thought to himself. Covering his eyes from the glare of the sun, he looked into the distance and spotted Nicky and Kwame sitting on a log. Kwame was smoking a cigarette and Nicky was gesticulating as he explained something to Kwame. Tony was too far away to hear their conversation, but it looked intense. Kwame didn't flinch as he absorbed everything that Nicky was telling him.

'I'm missing out on whatever is going on ... again!' Tony mumbled to himself. He got dressed hurriedly and made my way out to the spot that Kwame and Nicky had been sitting, but they had already left. He was now starting to feel ignored and isolated. Usually, Nicky would have woken him up or checked on him, as he would have done in return. They had spent so much time together and shared so many good memories. What was happening to Nicky? He was becoming distant and Tony didn't like it. Their bond was becoming strained by an unrecognisable tension of suspicion.

Tony wandered back towards the building and walked among the cages full of hens. He peered at the patas monkey, which seemed to be tame. It bounced calmly on it hind legs towards him with curious eyes, sniffing the air and licking its palm.

Tony hadn't seen a monkey like this before and he was fascinated by it. He looked closely at its brown eyes, its actions, the colour of its fur and markings, and most interestingly, the sound it was making. As he stood admiring the monkey, a lady appeared from the back of the building laughing.

'Don't be afraid, this is Appongo! He is the village pet. He won't hurt you!' She stretched her hand towards Tony and gave him a handful of nuts and seeds. 'Give these to him, then you will be able to touch him. He will climb on you but don't be frightened ... Appongo is playful!'

'Thank you!' replied Tony and opened his hand to receive the food.

'Teach! Teach!' A voice from behind him bellowed. 'We need to go on the road!' He turned around sharply to see Keto, Kwame, and Nicky standing at the corner of the building near his room window.

Tony passed the nuts back to the woman and apologised for having to go. He told her he hoped he would get another chance to experience the monkey's playfulness.

Tony turned quickly and walked towards the group. Nicky was in good spirits as he shouted, 'You must have slept like a baby...! We've been up since six!' His friend stepped forward and patted Tony on the back, who returned the gesture as the four men walked towards the waiting taxi and another car that was parked alongside. Kwame, Nicky and Tony occupied the taxi, which was followed by Keto along with two other local men.

As they set off, Kwame revealed that Keto was taking them to one of the locals who lived on the outskirts of Kinboasi. He said they would just pay him a visit today, so that they could show them what diamonds they have and so that payment could be worked out. Kwame also said that the Chief had already given this person some of the luxury items that they had brought with them. He said that they should be well received and shouldn't have to pay too much for the diamonds. After about ten minutes, they arrived at the wooden house, which had a small veranda with two wicker armchairs. The wooden floor was dyed dark red and the walls were painted a sunny yellow. Keto alighted from his car, knocked three times on the door and walked in the house. The three men came out of the taxi, leaving the locals outside in Keto's car. They followed Keto into the house, leaving the two local men seated in Keto's car. The house's owner was a grey-haired elderly slim woman. She spoke to Keto in their local dialect, before disappearing into another room. She then reappeared carrying a small rusty metal box, which she placed on her dining table.

Keto walked over to the table as she opened the box then removed a piece of calico, which she then unwrapped to reveal the contents of the box. Inside, there were about twenty stones of various sizes, shapes, and shades of crystal. Nicky and Tony looked at each other and their eyes widened. This was a lot more than they'd expected to find in one place. It appeared that the elderly lady had these stones for many years and had kept them hidden under strict instructions from the Chief. She had now decided to give up her collection. Keto and Kwame looked at the stones, separating the clearest and the biggest. Keto, Kwame and the elderly lady held discussion in their local dialect, seemingly negotiating the price. Keto had the last word and stroked the lady's back as he scooped up the selected stones and placed them in Kwame's hand.

Keto turned to Nicky and Tony; he acknowledged the receipt of the goods and told them that they would return later with the money to pay for the diamonds. They all left the house in astonishment and excitement. Keto indicated that they would visit another four houses today and continue until they had secured as many diamonds as possible. Tony wondered whether they would be able to take them all back to Weatherpool in one go. Keto also mentioned that the last day of the visit would be a day of rest and celebration. They would sacrifice the goats and hens that they'd seen at the local bed and breakfast. The whole community would be invited and each of the men would be tasked to kill one animal to protect them from any malevolence that may follow them out of the village.

The nights followed the days, and each day revealed more about their culture, the control exercised by the chief, and mist of secrecy that covered Kinboasi. It was clear that the community as a whole had an unimaginable wealth, but due to the world system that stipulate that diamonds must be Kimberley certified to attain market value, the people of Kinboasi and other similar communities would never yield the wealth that they should be entitled to. However, Kwame and his group had secured a huge quantity of diamonds, which would give them, and the diamond dealers of Watchmead Gardens, considerable fortune.

As they moved through the village and collected the diamonds, it became clear to Tony, that he and Nicky were not finding out how much Kwame and Keto were paying for the diamonds; in some cases it seemed as though they were taking diamonds without giving any money. In others, they seemed to give less than one hundred dollars for stones that were clearly worth tens of thousands of dollars back in Watchmead Gardens.

Tony enjoyed his time meeting with the local people and the food was always pleasurable. Their last day in Kinboasi had arrived and as Keto and Kwame had reiterated, the entire village came together for a feast. Nicky slaughtered one of the hens and Tony reluctantly killed one of the goats that he had gazed at through his window every morning. The local chefs came together to make a magnificent feast with all the trappings and delicacies; no parts of the animals or birds were wasted.

The heads and intestines of the goats were used to make a sumptuous soup, with mini dumplings, Okra, an assortments of local herbs and root vegetables. The limbs of the goat were chopped into small pieces. Some were cooked in a brown sauce, creating a sort of a stew. Most of the meat was cooked in spicy curried sauce, the local favourite. Meats were cooked until it was tender and on tasting it, each piece melted on the tongue. The caged hens feathers were plucked then the chicken was seasoned and roasted over an open wood fire. To add to the occasion of the feast, breadfruits were also roasted and fried. There were boiled yams, plantains, bananas and rice with peas and fufu to accompany the variety of meats. The celebration was in full swing and everyone was enjoying themselves immensely.

Whilst Keto and Tony enjoyed the occasion – the music, food, and culture – Nicky and Kwame were, again, nowhere to be seen. Keto whispered in Tony's ear as he realised that he was looking for the other men. 'Teach I have grown to respect you. You are not like Kwame and Nicky!' He paused and pull his chair closer. 'You should be careful about your friend Nicky. I shouldn't be the one to tell you this … but I don't think you should trust him.'

Keto's words shook Tony like an earthquake. He had felt that Nicky's attitude had changed recently. He no longer seemed to be the school friend he had known for so many years. He had hardened himself and drifted from Tony, damaging the bond that they'd had since childhood. Nicky's intentions were unclear, but Keto was very sure that Tony needed to be very careful. At the end of the event, Tony went to bed, not knowing where Nicky and Kwame were.

CHAPTER TEN

The vivid sunlight and brisk wind pricked Tony's eyelids as he woke up and looked out his window. It was the day after the feast and ceremonial celebration. The fragrances of the spices and the roasted meats still remained. Smoke rose from the ash in the wood lit fire at the back of the bed and breakfast where Appongo was still anchored to the bark of the fruit tree. He too had had a night of excitement as he entertained the locals with his many tricks, but, for now he was less playful. Exhausted, and with bits of food in his small hand, he was curled up on some tousled leaves next to some scraps of boiled yams and roasted breadfruit skin. As he fell into a deeper sleep he dropped some of the scraps onto the floor, which attracted a small group of lizards, who picked up the small pieces and scurried away.

Still looking out of the window, Tony took a deep breath as if to say goodbye to this place of tranquil beauty. In the back of his mind, I felt that, finally, everything was coming together. After all of his and Nicky's trials, he believed that, this time, they would have enough money to live the high life. Tony dreamed of giving up his job as a teacher. He wanted to enjoy life and maybe even move away from Weatherpool and Portland. It would be a new start for both of them.

Being the last to get up most days, Tony knew that today would probably not be any different. He got dressed and headed to the communal bar, where he saw Kwame talking with the server and counting some money.

'Hey Kwame!' Tony said, as he approached the bar and leaned against it. The bar was stained with alcohol from last night's event. Realising this,

Tony stepped away a little and checked his shirt for marks.

Kwame looked at him with no expression and nodded. 'All good, Teach?'

'Yes, I'm still getting over the feast. How about you?' 'Um ... yeah, I guess,' he replied, looking down at his watch. 'Keto and Nicky went on an early morning errand to get some fresh meat. They will be back soon!' He paused, then continued, 'We will go to the city, I mean Sanibo to meet up with the girls – get them ready for their flight!' He cleared his throat. 'I heard from the Chandler and Thaddeus's condition has improved slightly – he's stable – but he's still not out of the woods, as they would say!'

Tony's stomach turned on hearing this news. 'I hope he will recover soon!' he replied. 'How is the investigation going? Have they caught the culprit who attacked him?'

'No, they haven't as yet, but according to Chandler, they have cast a wide net of suspicion. They're investigating in many areas it seems.' Kwame reiterated that there were no witnesses, except for the child, but that the police believed he was with others performing a ritual when it all happened.

Worried, Tony kept his emotions hidden as he said goodbye to Kwame and walked away from the bar. He went to his room in an attempt to disguise his trepidation. If Thaddeus survives, it would be over for him and Nicky. If he's still alive when we they get back to Weatherpool, what should their next move be? Thoughts rattled through his mind as opened the door. He was just about to close it behind him when it burst back open. He jumped out of his skin in fear. 'What the f ....!!' he shouted.

'It's me, Kwame!'

Tony had only just left him at the bar, so it must have been an urgent reason for him to catch him up so quickly. Tony opened the door fully and Kwame pushed passed him, nearly knocking him over.

'I just came to make sure that you take everything! 'e mustn't leave anything behind!' he stressed, surveying the room as he spoke.

'Um!' Tony managed a part reply before

Kwame continued, 'Where's your bag?!'

'It's on the chair... in ...' Tony's words were interrupted by Kwame's insistence. He looked on as the man rushed around his room, probing and collecting together the few items that Tony had been using and packing them away in his bag. Kwame closed the zipper to Tony's holdall and handed it to him. Pondering at his actions, Tony took the holdall then remarked, 'Umm ... Could I not have done that myself??'

'Sorry, Teach!' Kwame replied, 'I just wanted to make sure that your room was clear and you're not leaving anything behind – you never know!' Kwame looked around again and checked underneath the mattress and the bed. It made Tony feel like he was being frisked ... to check whether he had any diamonds? Bizarre.

'Ok, let's go, quipped Kwame. ' Nicky and Keto should be back any minute!' We will go and get the girls ready.'

The plan was for Nicky to go with the girls and the diamonds back to Weatherpool, Portland. With Thaddeus still in hospital, he would go straight to

Bells and Bottoms with the girls to get the diamonds removed. Then, he would keep them until Kwame and Tony arrived at Fleming airport the following day. Nicky would pick them up with the diamonds and from there, they would go straight to Watchmead Gardens to meet with Mr Sheikhs and his sons.

Tony walked out first and Kwame followed slightly behind. He looked around the room again, before switching off the light and closing the door behind them. In the communal bar, Nicky and Keto were back from their excursion, sitting at a table with two hefty black plastic carrier bags. Both of the bags were bulging and sagging with the weight of the fresh animal meat.

Keto was first to greet Tony, 'Hey, Teach!' This was followed by Nicky, who said, 'You look ready to go, Teach!'

'Yeah, with a little help from Kwame ... yeah, I'm ready!' He'd made a slightly sarcastic joke, which was largely ignored. 'Bro, you look ready too!' he continued.

'Keto will come with us to get the girls ready

and help us with any problems on the way!'

Nicky patted Keto on the shoulder. 'He knows a lot of important people with the right connections to get us out of any sticky situations that we might get ourselves into!'

Keto looked at Kwame and mentioned that he got thirty kilograms of meat, as he wasn't sure how much would be needed. Keto opened one of the bags, taking credit for getting fresh cuts of lamb. He said it would make sure the packages place inside the dancers would stay intact during the journey, even with a lot of movement.

Keto continued and explained that he had people working in different departments of the airport. Out of the corner of his eye, Tony noticed the taxi driver carrying Kwame's suitcase from the corridor to his car. Kwame said nothing but walked to the side of the communal bar counter and went behind it, picking up a thin dark green holdall bag. The weight inside the bag was evident, as he switched the bag from his left to his right hand. He took the bag to the taxi and dropped it gently onto the floor in the front passenger foot well. It was clear that the contents of the bag made it heavy; in it was something metal. Kwame walked back to where the others stood and said that everything was ready and we should make our way. Kwame, Nicky, and Tony again went with the dedicated taxi driver in one car. Keto drove ahead in a separate car with two other local men. Tony noticed that they weren't leaving the village the same way as when they arrived. Instead of seeing roads lined with manicured orchards and groomed fruit trees, they drove through deserted, dry fields with unpaved roads; they went past cemeteries and ramshackle houses made from mud and timber. They hadn't visited this area during their five-day stay.

They continued for ten minutes before coming across an armed police check point. 'Oh, shit,' said Tony as Keto's car was stopped. Keto got out of his car, ignoring the waiting police officers. He picked up a notebook from his door pocket and walked back to the car in which Tony, Nicky and Kwame were sitting. He spoke to Kwame in their local language. Kwame replied angrily, hissing through his teeth before removing a stack of local bank notes from a small body pouch that he had slung across his chest.

Keto took the bank notes, increased them with some of his own, and recounted them; he then placed the unfolded notes into the open notebook and closed it before walking back and handing the book over to the waiting officers. He then got back into his car and set off again, followed dutifully by the taxi.

Relieved that, that was over, not that he knew what had happened, Tony sat back and they travelled for another three kilometres when they arrived at yet another armed checkpoint. It felt like they were going around in circles; the only difference with this checkpoint was that it had a small shack made from rusty zinc sheets. Keto alighted from the car again, his approach similar to before. However, this time he spoke with more authority to Kwame, who did not answer. Kwame gave Keto the pouch. Keto walked back to his car and carried out the same transaction as before.

They set off again on the unpaved road that cut through desolate plains littered with armed checkpoints, cemeteries, and wildlife scavenging on carcasses. There was no conversation; Nicky turned sideways looking blankly at the scenery and Kwame seemed focused on the bag that rattled whenever their car tyres hit a pothole. The journey seemed to be coming to an ending as their tyres eventually collided with asphalt surface, where, suddenly the landscape erupted with populated houses, streetlights, and pedestrian crossings.

'We should be there in few minutes!' said Kwame, speaking for the first time to Nicky and Tony since they had set off in the taxi. Still, Nicky said nothing.

'Ok.' replied Tony. He wondered why they had travelled on a different road to get to this point. It was odd. Perhaps the route was chose to ensure that they weren't ambushed by someone who knew they had the diamonds.

The taxi crawled into the carpark of a multi-storey hotel called The Paradise Hotel. The beautiful exterior was coated in bronze and had features carved into black marble tiles. Tony got out of the taxi, relieved at being able to stand up after the jolting ride; he looked up at the monument of civilisation. He picked up his backpack and flung it onto his shoulder, as he looked at the decorated car park and the immaculate garden that wrapped itself around the hotel.

'Teach!' insisted Kwame. 'Leave your bag in the car.'

'Ok!' replied Tony, taking it round to the boot.

Keto and his two passengers came over to where they stood. The men were carrying the two bags full of fresh meat. Kwame's driver then went to the booth to retrieve Kwame's suitcases. Kwame and Keto spoke and then headed towards the entrance of the hotel and into the lobby, where the impressive décor of opulence and elegance continued throughout. The reception desk was stacked with displays of brochures of tours and places of interest. The receptionists were both male and were smartly dressed in black suits and ties with grey shirts. There were waiting staff in white shirts, black bow ties and matching coloured trousers at the entrance to the Cabana restaurant and bar. Kwame and Keto approached the reception desk, leaving the rest of the party slightly behind as Kwame engaged in conversation with the receptionist, who typed away on the computer keyboard before handing Kwame some printed out pages. Kwame looked at the printed papers and asked for a pen as he scrutinised and haggled over the list and prices that were stated on the bills. It seemed that the girls had overspent. This discussion lasted longer than anyone had expected. The receptionist conceded and Kwame agreed and made payment with a bank card.

Keto instructed the two local men to hand over the bags of fresh meat to Tony and Nicky as they went back to wait in their car. Kwame spoke to Keto and the driver before leading the group to the shiny elevator, which was positioned to the left of the ornate reception desk. On the seventh floor, the dancers should be waiting for them in their rooms. Tony stepped into the elevator feeling happy that he and Nicky had worked hard and were on their way to collecting a significant amount of wealth that would lead to the lifestyle that they were desperate to experience full time.

The men exited the elevator and onto the seventh floor corridor. Kwame looked left, stepped forward, then stopped, backing into the group without apology, before walking down the right side corridor, counting the numbers as he went. He stopped at the end of the corridor in front of rooms 701 and 702. He pulled out two electronic keys and inserted one of the key cards into the lock and opened the door. He entered first, followed by Nicky, Keto, and Tony gestured for the driver to enter with the suitcases before following them in. The room was decorated beautifully with touches of gold and it had a balcony, the access to which was two tall glass doors, which were open. The room was messy. The girls had obviously enjoyed room service and there were empty bottles of wine, trays with plates of half-eaten food, and open cans of beer. Tony could see Jessica and Antonia sitting out on the balcony wearing two piece swimsuits.

Kwame walked through the sitting area of the room, knocking over some of the bottles as he passed between the sofas and the coffee table.

'Hey!!' Kwame shouted. 'We're here! I told you to be ready to get the job done and go to the airport!'

Jessica, the spunkier of the two, sprung to her

feet. 'We are ready to do as the boss told us!' referring to boss, Thaddeus. She barged passed Kwame, swinging her arms and hips rhythmically as she entered the room, shocked see the waiting entourage of five men, including Kwame. They all watched in bemusement as Kwame reinforced his authority in the absence of Thaddeus and the dancers succumbed.

Kwame instructed Jessica to go to the other room to get the other girls. The three came back within a minute, wearing as much as Jessica and Antonia. They discussed the process of cutting meat chunks and putting the diamonds inside them; Kwame went through the instructions for stitching the meat with cotton treading to secure the diamonds inside. With all of this established, the four dancers went into the bedroom. Kwame didn't trust them to do this on their own, so he insisted that the men would watch them pack the meat into their vaginas ready for the journey. The men all looked on with astonishment as the girls got to work. They didn't have the tools they had used at Bells and Bottoms with them this time, so it was nothing like the practice sessions they had a the strip club.

The process, which they had practised, now involved their hands, oils as lubricant, and petroleum jelly. The scene was pornographic, intense and impressive. The process took twenty minutes and throughout the dancers groaned and whimpered as the meat were pushed passed their gripping internal muscles. On finishing, the girls washed their hands, put on their underwear. As they got dressed, they kept moving their waist and bottoms to adjust their internal treasures into a comfortable position.

Although Nicky and Tony were very turned on by the experience, it was more than just selfish satisfaction. It meant wealth and control over a destiny that they are now in control of again. They looked at each other and nodded, communicating telepathically that they were almost there.

The girls looked stunning, and from a cultural perspective, they knew the dancers would have no problems getting through security checks, because they were women and Europeans. Nicky grabbed his backpack as the girls picked up their carry-on luggage and purses. 'It's time to go!' said Kwame. 'I'd asked the receptionist to organise a taxi to take five passengers to the airport in one hour, so the taxi should arrive soon, if it isn't here already.'

Kwame and Keto started to look around the room, opening all the drawers, pulling up the bedding, looking underneath the bed and behind to cushions in the sofa to see if the girls had left anything. They went into the second room and returned to say that all was good there. Looking satisfied, Kwame directed the dancers to the lift and the group of men followed. The lift could only accommodate five average sized people at a time, so Kwame and the dancers went first. Nicky, Tony, Keto, and the driver went next. They exited the elevator into the lobby, where the girls and Kwame were waiting.

'This is it bro!' Tony said to his friend.

'Yes, Teach!' He nodded 'I think this is really it!' They shook hands and patted each other on the back, giving each other a brotherly hug.

They stood back and watched the girls get into the waiting taxi. Kwame spoke to the driver and gave him the banknotes for their journey. Kwame walked towards Tony and said, sternly, 'Teach, where's your bag?'

Tony hesitated, wondering whether he had left it upstairs, but then remembered, 'It's in the taxi!' he pronounced.

'Ok!' replied Kwame. 'Let's go! We have just one more thing to do before we leave!'

They all walked towards the taxi, which was parked in the bay next to Keto's car. The two villagers were still sitting inside but one got out as they approached. One of the village men got into the taxi and sat in the seat previously occupied by Nicky, leaving Keto and the other to travel behind as the set off again. Tony realised that he had no idea where they were heading. They drove out of the city and after about twenty five minutes, turned off onto an unpaved road and continued, only stopped once the road was too narrow for a vehicle.

'Let's walk from here!' said Kwame. 'Walk where? asked Tony. His question ignored.

They left the cars behind; Kwame was in the lead and asked Tony to take his backpack and follow him closely. Tony noticed that the village man had picked up the thin dark-green holdall from the floor well at the front passenger seat, where it had rested at Kwame's feet since leaving the village. They walked for seven minutes on a dirt path, passing an abandoned diamond mine quarry that, over time, had naturally turned into a fishing pond. They then hiked up a hill, through a corn field, still in silence. Tony looked around him, starting to worry about what was going on. They climbed up a steep slope after passing a farmer's yam crop. They carried on walking under the shade of a huge oak tree. There was silence, stillness, no wind and the only faint sound of birds in distant tree-tops. Tony randomly thought it was strange that he couldn't hear any wildlife around them - a dead zone. He could hear Keto talking to another local man in the distance.

'Let's stop here!' said Kwame. The second villager placed the holdall on the vines and weeds and opened the zipper. He pulled out a shotgun and handed it to Kwame, who pointed it straight at Tony.

'Teach, this is why we're here!' said Kwame, looking at Tony down the barrel of the gun with a venomous look of hatred in his darkened eyes. He curled his lips as he continued, 'You think you are so smart, don't you, Teach? But you're not ... we got you figured out a long time ago!'

Tony felt numb. Had his best friend betrayed him after all? Had Nicky planned his demise with Kwame? Kwame walked towards Tony and pushed the shotgun into his chest. Tony could feel the cold metal through his shirt.

'Hold on a minute!' shouted a voice in the distance

How did he get end up on this path of life? Tony didn't want to die in this field. His thoughts unearthed an avalanche of emotions and memories. He remembered the bravery of his father standing next to his bed at three in the morning to protect him. Tony could still hear his father's voice. He could still see the bloodstains, and he could still see himself gazing blankly into his neighbour's mirror.

'Hey, it's me ... it's Tony! Do you know where Nicky and Marianna are?'

Printed in Poland
by Amazon Fulfillment
Poland Sp. z o.o., Wrocław

65414739R00167